U0165459

30 週年暢銷紀念版・中英雙語

星星婆婆的雪鞋

Two Old Women

馴鹿民族流傳兩千年的勇氣傳說

Velma Wallis

威兒瑪・瓦歷斯｜著　　王聖棻・魏婉琪｜譯

馴鹿民族的命運與勇氣

呂政達（作家）

首先，做一個選擇題。你認為，什麼樣的女人，特別吸引人？一、有權力的女人；二、美麗的女人；三、富有的女人；四、聰明的女人。

你想，這幾個答案，大概已包含女性吸引人的特質了。然而，試想很久以前，遙遠的阿拉斯加，兩個遭族人拋棄、在雪地荒野求生的老婆婆，沒有權力，容貌蒼老，既無恆產，也缺乏驚人的經歷事蹟，卻為什麼自這本書問世以來，經過讀者的閱讀、相傳，成為某種令人神往的女性典範？

當你開始讀這本書，追尋星月下兩個老婆婆的雪地蹤跡時，這個問題，將反覆在你腦海翻湧、浮現。你不可能照單全收故事裡古老的求生技巧，獵捕松鼠、柳樹松雞和野兔，或真的有意學習拋擲手斧、泅入冰凍河水捕魚、生火。薰習資本主義商品交易邏輯的社會裡，這些情節描繪，只會是不合時宜的異國風味，或遠處的民族寓言，已經足夠讓我們動容。然而，穿透故事表象，讀者將能體會「生存」以及其本身彰顯的意志，已經足夠讓我們動容。

正如威兒瑪・瓦歷斯透過莎，較年輕的那個婆婆所說的：「我的意志力比我的身體知覺還要強大。」這句話，從原始洞窟到現代職場，在所有人類群聚型態裡，都可輕易找到擁護者，也可輕易成為艱難處境時的救贖。

把這個故事當成警世寓言，威兒瑪・瓦歷斯告訴讀者兩個道理，一是為了生存，人可以做出殘忍的事，降到像狼群拋棄病狼那般的動物本能，甚至觸犯吃人的禁忌。

然而，也是為了生存，也可以做出高貴的事。像故事裡兩個老婆婆的互助、友情、勇氣與激發潛能。放棄努力而死去是比較容易的，但活下去並不是「為了向任何人證明什麼」，「生存」就是意志與智慧最好的證明。

威兒瑪・瓦歷斯是阿拉斯加的哥威迅人，近代史裡，這個有著「馴鹿民族」封號的族群，本身多次徘徊在文明入侵、滅絕與消逝的危機裡，二○○三年，美國國會還否決布希政府開發馴鹿最後棲息地的龐大計畫，當年，哥威迅人的領導者成為挽救生態的戰士。事實上，從這本早十年出版的故事書裡，我們就已預見馴鹿民族的命運與勇氣。雪地上兩個老婆婆的微小身影，竟然就是這個游獵部落的縮影——現代文明要拋棄他們，為了開發和商機趕盡殺絕，而說不定，哥威迅人早就從這則流傳千年的口語傳奇裡，學習到面對強權的意志與勇氣。生存，就是一切的開始。

有位北美的原住民作家曾說，每個印第安人聽來的故事，都可以寫成書。

威兒瑪·瓦歷斯則是真的將媽媽講給她聽的故事，寫成動人的雪地篇章。建議有興趣的讀者還可找她接著寫的《Raising Ourselves: A Gwich'in Coming of Age Story from the Yukon》一讀，這本書是她從傳奇故事轉入現實的自傳性作品，更具體細微地描寫了阿拉斯加人面對現代文明入侵的種種心情與調適。你還可以讀到媽媽跟她講《星星婆婆的雪鞋》故事時，那棟只有兩個房間，卻擠滿十三個兄弟姊妹的小屋，以及父母為了餵飽他們的各種奮鬥經過。然後，你才會真的體會，為什麼在她的作品裡，生存是如此重要的一件事。

你喜歡這個女人嗎？

為了延續愛與生命的艱苦奮鬥

收到這本書的試閱時，我一看簡介，就有極大的興趣，因為故事的內容發生在我非常非常喜愛的阿拉斯加，故事的角色就是阿拉斯加的原住民。我放下手邊的工作，馬上就開始閱讀。

這是一個樸實又感人的故事，在目前很多小說都強調故事要反轉又反轉，懸疑又刺激，這個故事則是去除掉過多膩人的調味料，用原汁原味的情感來傳遞簡單的感動。

這本書的作者威兒瑪‧瓦歷斯是阿拉斯加的哥威迅人原住民，出生成長於內阿拉斯加一個小城鎮──育空堡。那是一個沒有公路可以到達的城鎮，只有靠飛機、狗雪橇、船，或步行才能抵達。我跟先生曾在二○二二年在阿拉斯加自駕五十二日行，見識到那片廣大土地的特殊景觀，很多地方即便不是島嶼也沒有公路到達，甚至是首都朱諾也一樣，沒有過度的開發，這讓阿拉斯加保留很多的自然野生景觀。

這個故事來自作者的母親，是族裡口耳相傳的古老故事，講述在西方文明未到達前，哥威迅人在嚴峻環境下生存時面對的選擇。有為了維繫更多族人的命運而不得不的遺棄，有面對背叛的絕望心情，有挑戰困境的不放棄，還有更多更深沉的感情在書中描述。

閱讀這個故事，對我來說，又有更深一層的意義，它更深刻印證我們在阿拉斯加五十二日行中對原住民生活接觸的印象。像是第二章一開始簡短提到不讓火熄滅的蕈，學名叫木蹄層孔菌（*Fomes fomentarius*），英文俗名是「Tinder Conk」。在沒有電、沒有瓦斯的年代，當地居民利用這種長在樹上的馬蹄型蕈類來當火種傳遞工具，他們會在乾燥的蕈殘渣塞回洞口，再用挖出來的蕈殘渣塞回洞口，餘燼可以在裡面維持緩慢燃燒的狀態好幾天。阿拉斯加的原住民就是用這種方式把火種從一個地方帶到另一個地方，從一個部落帶到另一個部落。當時我在阿拉斯加看到很多，也收集一個帶回家紀念，這次在書中閱讀到故事主角實際使用，可以看到他們是如何聰明地善用大自然。

我們當時去的時候是夏天，就如書上所描述，當地原住民在這個季節非常的忙碌，他們必須努力打獵、捕魚，做好燻鮭魚、乾肉，這一切都是為了漫長的冬天做準備。書中的年歲是千百年前，現在他們的生活加入現代化的房子、車子和工具，但是本質上的步調還是如此。

相應於這個故事，我們曾在一個屋子前看到一名獵人帶回好幾頭馴鹿，他跟兩個男孩一起切割鹿肉時，我們上前和他們聊天。他有點靦腆，但還是友善又熱情地分享他的故事，只是不准我們拍照。他告訴我們，他們會先把肉分給族裡面的老人家跟寡婦，最後才是自己和家人享用。他也會這樣教導孩子們，以後也會這樣傳承下去。不管是哪個故事，都有它發生的背景跟必然的現象，沒有必要批判或比較。但是我們都可以從中感受到這些民族為了在這片廣大又艱苦的土地上生存所要做的努力跟奮鬥，不管用什麼方法，保護族人、讓族人生命延續都是最大的考量。

一本關於生存，關於感情，關於勇氣的書。值得閱讀。

一個關於勇氣、背叛與生存的傳說

喻小敏（文化總會副祕書長）

《星星婆婆的雪鞋》故事開始於價值的衝突，而衝突則凸顯事情的本質。

兩個老婆婆遭遺棄後，突破冰天雪地、年老體衰、食物短缺等逆境，強調「奮力一搏」的堅強生命力，打破了社會的偏見，重新賦予老人尊重與社會價值。

更重要的是，作者瓦歷斯更從親情、友情等情感上著墨，不斷鋪陳群體對於個人的重要性。故事最後，當小孫子來跟老婆婆要回小手斧、羞愧的女兒和母親相擁而泣的畫面，更讓人為之動容，久久不已。

如此動人心魄的北方傳奇故事，一九九七年在台灣初次登場時就獲得許多讀書會、團體的廣泛討論，圖書館借閱率也相當高；期待野人文化《星星婆婆的雪鞋》的重新出發，能讓更多讀者從書中體會主人翁歷經被族人背叛、重新找回自己、建立友情、克服不信任感等澎湃洶湧的心路歷程，重新挖掘人生價值的強度與力度。

殘酷環境中的逆向思考

劉克襄（作家）

在殘酷的天地間，面對蒼老、衰弱的身子，以及逐漸到來的死亡威脅，毋寧是悲哀的。本書以此逆向敘述，透過兩位老婦人日常生活細節的應對，深入地刻劃一個族群的自然傳統文化，無疑是最值得反覆深思的重要內涵。

故事是年長者送給年輕人的禮物

王聖棻、魏婉琪（本書譯者）

哥威迅人稱威兒瑪·瓦歷斯為「娜印」（naa'in），意為「住在矮樹叢裡的女人」，表示一個離開部落生活圈子，只能從矮樹叢裡往外看的人。

瓦歷斯一九六〇年出生於內阿拉斯加，一個人口僅有六百五十人的偏遠村莊——育空堡，那是一個只有船、雪車、狗雪橇和飛機能到達的地方。她生長在一個傳統的阿撒巴斯卡家庭中，兄弟姊妹共有十三人。父親在她十三歲時去世，之後她輟學幫助母親撫養年紀尚輕的弟妹。因為個性怯懦，沒有再回去上學，因此在族人眼中，她是一個不屬於部落生活圈當中的人。十八歲時，瓦歷斯在親友訝異的眼光中，一個人搬到離村莊將近二十公里遠的小屋，那是她父親設陷阱用的地方。她斷斷續續獨自住在那裡達十二年之久，並且學習狩獵和設陷阱的技巧，以傳統阿撒巴斯卡人的生活方式維生。

寫下自己部落的傳奇故事

出於對閱讀的熱忱，她通過高中同等學力測驗，也在哥哥的教導下，學會如何打字。她前往育空堡的阿拉斯加大學分校，借了一部電腦，就此開始她說故事的生涯。她的第一個文學寫作計畫便是將母親告訴她，關於兩個被拋棄的老婆婆如何掙扎求生的傳奇故事寫下來。這個故事變成她的第一本書。

《星星婆婆的雪鞋》取材自一則阿撒巴斯卡母女間口耳相傳兩千多年的傳奇故事。這支阿拉斯加北極地區的游獵部落，遭遇到嚴冬最無情的考驗，他們必須遷移，並考量整個部落的生存，酋長決定把平時只會抱怨、為部落貢獻價值愈來愈少的兩個老婆婆留下。

契日婭和莎騾然失去部落的照顧、生存的資源，遭到親人的背叛，只帶著孫子給的一把斧頭和不屈服的尊嚴，努力度過寒冬，重新找回她們遺忘的力量和堅強。

故事中所描述的族群，是散居在目前育空堡和查爾基齊克區域的哥威迅人部落的一支，哥威迅人則是阿拉斯加的阿撒巴斯卡十一個不同部落中的一個。阿撒巴斯卡人散布在阿拉斯加內陸，大部分居住於布魯克斯山脈和阿拉斯加山脈之間。許多阿撒巴斯卡人不僅能通曉其他部落的語言，更和納瓦約與阿帕契印第安部落的語言有著相同的語源。一般認為，所有印第安人都是在冰河時期之初，跨越東西伯利亞進入阿拉斯加的亞洲人。

遺棄老人也許在現代社會是令人難以接受的行為，但在阿撒巴斯卡人生活的嚴酷環境中，這卻是「犧牲少數，保全多數」的不得已選擇。阿撒巴斯卡人必須根據季節變化，在一些預料可能豐收的漁獵地點紮營。土地常常無法提供足夠的食物給部落，飢荒的可能性是眾所周知的現實。

因此瓦歷斯用簡單生動的文字，描述這兩個遙遠冰雪大地上不肯被命運擊倒的老婆婆，也並未對遺棄她們的族人有過多苛責，只將重點放在老婆婆的智慧、韌性，以及部族故事的傳承上。瓦歷斯認為「故事是年長者送給年輕人的禮物」，但如今部族的年輕人被電視及現代生活的快速步調占據，這個「禮物」也不再像以前那樣收送頻繁。她希望寫下這些故事，能讓年輕族人更了解自己與傳統的聯繫，了解過去，也因此更了解自己。

一波三折的出版過程

然而，《星星婆婆的雪鞋》的出版之路，一開始並不順遂。

一開始是資金短缺。一九八九年瓦歷斯將草稿交給 Epicenter Press，當時這個出版社正在草創時期，難以支出龐大的印刷費用。出版社的發起人兼本書的編輯，同時也任教於阿拉斯加大學的拉耶兒‧摩根（Lael Morgan），將這個故事拿給學生傳閱，她的學生出於對這個故事的真心喜愛，自願發起募款，希望能經由獨立出版的方式將這本書付梓。在 Epicenter Press 終於成長到足以發行這本書時，他們已經募集了兩千美元。

出乎意料之外，這本書一開始並沒有受到族人的支持。瓦歷斯將部落裡傳承已久的故事，以文字的方式呈現在「外人」面前，所開啟的一扇文化大門不僅通往部落外的世界，也通向許多阿拉斯加人的生活，只是並不是所有人都喜歡那扇通往外界的門。一位在阿拉斯加原住民語言中心擔任翻譯的部落長者凱瑟琳‧彼得（Katherine Peter）就說：「把故事賣出去，就像是把你的遺產賣給別的國家。」

瓦歷斯自己也在一場村落舉辦的讀書會中感受到這股阻力，她發現雖然大多數人都很用心聆聽，卻可以感覺到有些村民對於她所朗讀的內容震驚莫名。甚至有人匿名向報紙抱怨，說瓦歷斯沒有權利以「她那種方式」描述哥威迅人。在一位部落領導人威爾‧瑪友（Will Mayo）對於出版這本書持反對意見之後，這本書的出版工作幾乎停擺。「這本書也許會引起爭議，因為它描述的是一種非常不道德的情況，會有許多人在對於我們族人沒有任何概念的情況下看到這本書，而我不確定哥威迅人會喜歡書裡的描述……」瓦歷斯自己對於族人的反對深感驚訝：「那就像是揭開了某種神祕面紗，而人們並不喜歡自己的面紗被揭開。」

所幸並非所有人都持反對態度。南西・詹姆斯（Nancy James）是前任育空堡市長，也是部落的領導人，她對於瓦歷斯的書感到驕傲。她表示，由哥威迅人來說哥威迅人的故事是最好的。其他人也許只是忌妒瓦歷斯，或是任何一個在外面世界功成名就的人。瓦歷斯則表示：「一旦故事用紙張記錄下來，有些故事會很樂意被當成是歷史，只是故事也許並非事實……每個文化都有自己的故事，難道糖果屋的故事會比較不恐怖嗎？在古老的游牧部落中，不只是遺棄，連食人這樣的事情也曾經發生。」

傳頌不斷的愛

也許是因為瓦歷斯的堅定意志。經過《安克拉治日報》（The Anchorage Daily News）針對這個問題大幅報導，以及其他媒體如「美聯社」（Associated Press）節錄書中故事刊載，當一九九三年九月本書出版時，整個阿拉斯加地區都引頸期盼這本書的發行。所謂「時勢造英雄」，由於當時美國文壇對於原住民文學的熱切渴望，這本書一上市便銷售一空，之後再版、三版，熱潮依然不退。除了紐約的大出版商 Haper Collins 買下平裝本版權，這本書也陸續在世界各國，以十七種語言文字出版上市。瓦歷斯因而一躍成為百萬作家，只是她不希望讓族人認為自己是藉由部落的故事來牟利，因此她只拿了區區五千五百美元的稿酬。

除了市場上的肯定，本書榮獲一九九三年美國西部州際圖書獎、最佳原創非小說類獎，同時也是一九九四年西北太平洋書商協會獎得主。

從本書裡，我們不僅可以看到昔日阿撒巴斯卡人的生活方式，更提到許多關係到現代人的事情，例如老人在養老院或退休社區裡被遺棄、被隔離的問題；或是老人一方面認為自己經驗豐富，一方面卻又低估自己還有能力的問題。在今日逐漸老年化的社會中，老人的照顧、醫療等問題正逐漸浮現，要解決這些問題，可說是相當棘手。但也許答案就在本書之中，如作者瓦歷斯所說：「也許明天的世代也會懂得知道這樣的故事，他們或許能夠更了解過去的事情，也希望能幫助他們了解自己……這個故事告訴我，不論什麼年齡，只要出於必須，一個人在生活中實現事物的能力是無窮的。」

代代傳遞的禮物

每天砍完柴，我們會坐在波丘派恩河口的小帳篷裡聊天，也就是與育空河交會的河口岸邊。我們總是以母親說的故事作為聊天的句點（即使現在我已經離年輕歲月很遠了，我的母親還是會為我說床邊故事！）有天晚上，我初次聽到這個故事——關於兩個老婆婆，以及他們度過重重難關一路走來的故事。

會想起這個故事，是因為之前有一次在搜集冬天要用的木頭時，我和母親的對話。我們坐在鋪蓋捲上，對於母親在五十出頭的年紀還能做這麼辛苦的工作嘖嘖稱奇，因為和她同年紀的人，大多數都已經因為年老和一些其他問題而卸下了工作。我告訴她，等我老了以後也要和她一樣。

我們開始回想過去的光景。以前，我的祖母和其他長者總是讓自己保持忙碌，直到他們無法行動自如或過世。母親自豪於能夠克服年老的一些困境，並且仍然可以搜集冬天要用的木頭，雖然事實上就身體來說，這項工作很困難，有時候根本難以忍受。母親想起了這個特別的故事，因為它正好契合我們當時心裡的想法和感覺。

後來，我在我們過冬的小屋中將這個故事寫下來。我對這個故事印象很深刻，因為它不僅教導了我可以應用在生活中的一課，更重要的是，這個故事和我的族人以及我的過去息息相關──那是我能夠緊緊抓住，並且稱它是「屬於我」的事情。故事是年長者送給年輕人的禮物。可惜的是，在今日，這個禮物不再像以前那樣收送頻繁，因為許多年輕人被電視以及現代生活的快速步調所占據。也許明天，這個世代的一些人能夠有充分的敏感度，傾聽長者的智慧，而這些人也會在記憶裡擁有傳統口耳相傳的故事。也許下一個世代也會得知像這樣的故事，他們或許能夠更了解過去，也希望能幫助他們了解自己。

這兩個老婆婆的故事發生的時間遠早於西方文化傳入，而且一直在世代之間流傳，在人與人之間傳遞，傳到我的母親，再傳到我。雖然我在寫這個故事的時候，用了一點點自己創造出來的想像，但這的的確確是我母親告訴我的故事，而且故事的重點仍然和母親希望我能聆聽的用意一樣。

這個故事告訴我，不論什麼年齡，只要出於必須，一個人在生活中實現事物的能力是無窮的。在這個廣大複雜的世界中，每個人都有令人驚異的巨大潛能。但是除非命運的安排，這些隱藏的禮物極少被帶到現實生活之中。

目次

擔心這樣的死亡會遠遠超過我們所經歷的任何痛苦，所以即使我們終將要死，我們也要奮力一搏！

她們從製作雪鞋開始，但她們沒有適當的工具，只能利用手邊現有的東西將每根木頭劈成四條，再放到以白樺木製成的大容器裡煮沸。

她們又再一次讓自己的身體超過負荷。莎不由自主發出痛苦的吶喊，感受到一股想大哭一場的衝動。她抱著頭，想到這些日子以來經歷的一切，覺得自己完全被擊潰了，而四周的寒冷讓她更加絕望。不管怎麼努力，身體就是不肯動一下。

她們得在白天多找點事來做。只是，即使兩個老婆婆讓自己忙於工作，仍然可以感覺到一股巨大的寂寞感，慢慢地將她們團團包圍。

第一章
飢寒交迫

嚴酷的、寂靜的、冷冽的空氣在這片遼闊的土地鋪展開來。高聳的雲杉積著厚重的白雪，靜靜等待來自遠方的春風吹拂。如此的寒冷，就連結霜的柳樹似乎都在顫抖著。

這片看似悲苦的土地上，遠處有一群身穿動物皮毛的人，正緊緊圍著一個小小的火堆取暖。他們飽經風霜的臉龐，此時因飢餓而更顯絕望，未來，一片渺茫。

這支游獵部落是阿拉斯加北極地區的原住民，總是馬不停蹄尋找食物。只要是馴鹿和其他遷徙動物所到之處，就有他們的足跡。但是這個嚴峻酷寒的冬天，卻出現了不同於以往的問題。麋鹿一向是他們最中意的食物來源，但是為了避開刺骨的寒冷，麋鹿選擇待在原地不動，要找到牠們變得格外困難；而體型較小、容易捕捉的動物，像是兔子和野松鼠之類，又不足以填飽整個部落的肚子，尤其是像他們這種大型部落。這麼冷的天氣，就算是小動物也躲得不知所蹤，不然就是因為人類或其他動物的捕捉而變得稀少。在這不尋常的深秋苦寒時節，由於寒意無情的肆虐，整片土地彷彿生機盡失。

在嚴寒中打獵，需要比平常更多的體力，所以有食物總是獵人先吃，因為整個部落都仰賴他們的狩獵技巧生存。可是有這麼多獵人等著填飽肚子，捕獲的獵物一下子就消耗殆盡。雖然他們已經盡了最大的努力出外獵捕，女人和小孩仍為營養不良的問題所苦，甚至死於飢餓。

在這特別的一群人裡，有兩個經年受到部落照顧的老婆婆。老一點的那個名叫契日婭，因為她的出生讓她的父母聯想到一種稱做契卡地的山雀。另外一個婆婆名叫莎，意思是星星，因為她出生的時候，母親仰望秋夜天空遠方的星星出神，而忘了分娩時劇烈收縮的疼痛。

每當部落遷徙到一個新的營地，酋長就會指示年輕小夥子為這兩位老婆婆安置好居住的地方，並且將木柴和水交給她們。較年輕的女人會將兩人的家當拖到新營地，她們則為那些幫忙的人鞣皮作為回報。這種安排一直以來都相安無事。

但是，和當時的族人相比，這兩個老婆婆共同有個不太尋常的特點。她們常常抱怨這裡痛那裡痛，而且總是隨身帶著枴杖，好證明自己所言不虛。奇怪的是，部落裡的人並不以為意，即使大家從小學到的真理是，住在這片險惡嚴峻的土地上，軟弱是不被允許的。沒有人責怪她們，她們也不斷地跟著身強體壯的人四處游獵，直到命運的那一天來臨。

那天，空氣中除了寒冷，還多了一絲特殊氣氛，所有族人都圍繞在冒出零星火花的火堆旁，聆聽酋長說話。他站起來比其他人高了將近一個頭，身穿毛皮外衣，戴著毛茸茸的頭套，對眾人說明接下來的日子會有多冷、多艱難，以及如果要順利過冬，大家應該要做些什麼。

接著他突然用洪亮的聲音宣布一件事。「長老會議和我已經做了決定，」「我們要把老人留下酋長停頓了一下，似乎在為接下來要所說的話尋找力量，來。」

他很快地掃視了一下群眾，看看他們有什麼反應，但是大家只關心飢餓和寒冷，似乎沒有太震驚。許多人早就猜到會發生這件事，還有人覺得這是對部落最有利的決定。在當時，碰到飢荒就把老人棄之不顧並不駭人聽聞，只是在這個部落還是第一次發生。生活在這片嚴酷的土地上，似乎迫使人們模仿動物的某些行為，以便能夠存活，就像年輕有能力的狼群會離開老狼王一樣；這些人把年老的人留下，就可以移動得更快，沒有多餘負擔。

那個比較老的婆婆契日婭，她的女兒和孫子也在人群之中。酋長在人群裡看到他們，卻發現他們也沒有什麼特別的反應。能夠順利宣布這件不愉快的決定，酋長鬆了一大口氣，他隨即指示眾人立刻整理行囊。同時，這位身為部落領導者的勇敢男人，卻無法正視這兩位老婆婆，因為他覺得當下自己還沒有那麼堅強。

酋長很清楚為什麼部落裡關心她們的人沒有反對這件事。在這艱困的時候，許多男人都變得煩躁易怒，只要說錯或做錯一件事，就可能引起一陣騷動，讓事情變得更糟糕。所以，部落裡的老弱婦孺只能將自己心中的不愉快隱藏起來，因為他們知道，寒冷會為這群掙扎求生的人帶來恐慌，進而引發殘忍野蠻的行為。

許多年來，老婆婆一直和部落共進退，酋長也一直受到她們的關愛。現在他只想盡快離開，這樣她們就不會看著他，讓他的心情一直處在人生最低潮。

兩個老婆婆坐在營火前，顯得年邁而瘦小，她們驕傲地將下巴抬高，以掩飾心中的震驚。在她們年輕的時候也看過很多老的人被部落拋棄，但是沒想到這樣的命運也會降臨在自己身上。她們眼光呆滯地望著前方，彷彿沒有聽到酋長所宣判的死刑。這等於是被單獨留在一個只承認力量的土地上，自食其力、自生自滅。兩個脆弱的老婆婆面對這樣的遊戲規則，可以說一點機會都沒有。酋長宣布的消息讓她們無言以對，也沒有辦法保護自己。

兩個老婆婆中，契日婭是有家庭的人，她有一個女兒，名叫歐姿希‧內麗，還有個孫子旭盧勃‧祖。她等著女兒出聲抗議，但女兒卻一聲不吭，讓她更是深受打擊，竟然連自己的女兒都沒試著保護她。一旁的莎也驚訝得目瞪口呆。

契日婭的腦袋一團混亂，她想大叫，一個字也發不出聲；她覺得自己好像身處一場可怕的噩夢中，無法動彈也不能言語。

部落的人慢慢啟程離開，契日婭的女兒走向她母親，手上提著一捆皮條，那是撕成細條狀的厚生麋鹿皮，具多種用途。契日婭的女兒羞愧而悲傷地垂著頭，因為母親對她視而不見。契日婭無懼地望著前方。

歐姿希‧內麗完全不知所措。她很害怕如果站出來幫媽媽說話，部落裡的人會以此為由，將她和她的兒子也一起拋棄。更糟的是，大家都在挨餓，他們也許會做出更殘暴的事。她不能冒險。

帶著這些恐懼的想法，歐姿希‧內麗慢慢將皮條放在臉色凝重的母親面前，靜靜地以哀傷的眼神希望求得寬恕與諒解。然後她慢慢轉身，心中滿是悲痛地走開，她心裡明白，就在剛剛，自己已經失去了母親。

契日婭的孫子旭盧勃‧祖，對於這種殘忍的事相當不以為然。他是個不平凡的男孩。當其他男孩忙著打獵和摔角，比賽誰比較有男子氣概時，旭盧勃‧祖卻樂意幫助他的媽媽，以及兩個老婆婆。他的行為似乎跟這個部落世代相傳的生活習慣大相逕庭。傳統上，女人要做大部分的粗活，像是拖拉那些結實打包的平底雪橇。此外，大多數費時的工作也習慣由女人來做，男人主要專心在打獵上，如此整個部落才能生存下去。沒人為此抱怨，因為事情就是這樣，而且一直如此。

旭盧勃‧祖一直很敬重女人。他目睹她們如何被對待，他無法認同。雖然很多人跟他解釋了無數次，旭盧勃‧祖仍不明白，為什麼男人不能幫女人。他所受的教誨告訴他，絕對不准質疑部落長久以來的行事方式，因為那是不尊重。但當他還小的時候，他可是一點都不怕把這方面的疑問說出來，因為年幼無知就是他的擋箭牌。等到長大了些，他才知道這樣的行為會招來處罰。靜默的處罰讓他痛苦萬分，即使是媽媽也會好幾天不和他說話。所以旭盧勃‧祖了解到，有些事情最好不要說出來，放在腦袋裡想比較不會痛苦。

雖然覺得拋棄無助的老婆婆是部落最不應該做的事，旭盧勃‧祖卻為此掙扎不已。他的媽媽在他眼中看到即將爆發的怒氣，知道他快要出聲抗議。歐姿希‧內麗很快來到他的身邊，在耳邊低聲要他別想這件事，因為部落裡的男人已經很不高興，隨時都可能做出殘忍的舉動。旭盧勃‧祖看到部落男人陰沉的臉色，知道媽媽所言不虛，他緊緊抿著嘴不出聲，即使他的心仍然激動難抑地狂跳著。

當時，每個男孩都被教導要好好照料自己的武器，有時候照顧武器比照顧自己所愛的人還要周到，因為當他長大成人，所有生計都仰賴這把武器。如果一個男孩被人發現拿武器的方式錯誤，或是拿武器去做別的事，就會受到嚴厲懲罰。當男孩長大，他會知道這把武器的威力以及重要性，不僅關乎他個人的生存問題，還關係到整個部落的存活。

旭盧勃‧祖將平日的訓練以及自己的安全問題，全都拋到九霄雲外。他把自己的短柄小斧從腰帶上解下來。這把斧頭是以動物骨頭磨利製成的，上面緊緊纏著經過強化的皮條。他偷偷把斧頭藏在一棵樹枝濃密的幼雲杉上，巧妙避開部落眾人的眼光。

當旭盧勃‧祖的媽媽打包行李時，他轉身走向祖母。契日婭似乎一眼就看穿他的想法，旭盧勃確定旁邊沒有人注意，對著祖母指一指他的空腰帶，再指

一指雲杉。

旭盧勃再度望著祖母，眼神充滿絕望，不情願地轉身走回其他人身邊，心中強烈希望自己能夠做些神奇的事情，結束這可怕的一天。

飢餓的部落人群逐漸散去，只留下兩個老婆婆還坐在堆起來的雲杉樹枝上。她們錯愕地待在原地，微弱火光在她們飽經滄桑的臉龐映出一片淡淡的橙色。過了許久，寒冷才讓契日婭回過神來。她想起女兒臉上無奈的表情，但是她依然認為，她唯一的孩子應該不畏危險，挺身為她說話。她想到孫子，又不禁心軟了。她怎麼可以把這麼痛苦的情緒加在一個如此年輕、體貼的人身上呢？但是其他人讓她感到憤怒，特別是女兒！難道自己沒有教導女兒要堅強嗎？她不由地流下熱淚。

莎抬起頭，正好看見契日婭的淚水，胸中充滿怒氣。他們竟敢這麼做！被羞辱的情緒讓她的臉頰如火燒般滾燙。她們兩個又不是快死了！難道她們沒有盡力鞣製縫補族人交付的皮革嗎？而且其他人又不需要載著她們倆在營地間移動。她們既非毫無用處，也不是希望全無，但依然被判了死刑。

莎的朋友已經歷過八十個夏天，她呢，則是七十五個。年輕的時候，她看到被拋棄的老人都是離死亡不遠的人，大多瞎了，而且無法行走。現在呢？她還能走動，眼睛還看得見，嘴巴還能說話，但是……哼！現在的年輕人只想找簡單的方法度過難關。冷風吹熄了營火，莎的心中卻燃起一團更熾熱的火焰，就像是火堆餘燼迎著風，再度散發光亮般。她走到雲杉樹旁，取下那把斧頭，想到她朋友的孫子，不禁面露微笑。她走向朋友，嘆了一口氣，她的朋友依然文風不動。

莎抬頭看著蔚藍的天空。從她經驗豐富的眼睛看出去，這種冬天的藍色代表寒冷，等到夜晚降臨，很快會變得更冷。她因為擔憂而皺著眉，在契日婭身旁蹲下來，用一種溫和卻堅定的聲音對她說：「我的朋友，」她停頓了一下，希望能感受到更多力量，「我們可以坐在這裡等待死亡降臨，我們不會等太久的⋯⋯」

「我們離開這個世界的那一刻應該不遠了，」莎的朋友抬起頭看著她，眼中帶著驚恐，她很快繼續說下去，「但是如果只坐在這裡等待，我們必死無疑。這只會證明我們的確毫無用處。」

契日婭絕望地聽著她說話。她知道她的朋友幾乎已要接受因為寒冷和飢餓而死亡的命運。莎的語氣更為迫切：「是的！在他們看來，他們已經宣告我們的死亡！他們認為我們太老，毫無用處，忘了我們也有生存下去的權利！所以我認為，即使終將會死，我的朋友啊，我們也要奮力一搏，而非坐以待斃。」

第二章

奮力一搏

契日婭靜靜地坐著，似乎正試著整理混亂的思緒。當她聽完朋友一席強而有力的話，原本一片黑暗的內心，燃起一點希望的火花。寒冷正刺痛著剛剛淚水流過的地方，她傾聽著族人離開後留下的一片寂靜。她知道朋友剛剛說的話一點都沒錯，如果不為自己做點什麼，那麼在這片寧靜寒冷的土地上，肯定也只有死亡等待著她們。雖然心裡的絕望仍然多於堅定，但她終於開口回應：

「好，我們要試過所有方法才死。」說完這句話，她的朋友扶著她從濕透的樹枝堆上站起來。

她們收集一些樹枝，生起火堆，並添加一些薑片讓火不會熄滅，這種薑會在倒塌的灰楊樹上大片生長並乾枯。她們將部落中其他還沒熄滅的火堆餘燼收集起來。

當遷徙的部落整理出發裝備時，他們會將火紅的木炭儲存在強化過的麋鹿皮囊或是樺樹皮的容器中，裡面裝滿餘燼熄滅之後的灰，以便快速生起下一堆營火。

夜晚即將到來，她們從整捆皮條中抽出幾條切細，再將其打成套索，大小正好與兔子的頭一樣。雖然疲憊不堪，她們仍然打算設置一些捕兔的陷阱，並且立刻動身去布置。

橙色的月亮掛在地平線的那一端，看起來非常巨大。她們艱困地穿越深度及膝的雪地，藉著微弱的光線尋找兔子活動的痕跡。要看清楚已經相當困難，更不用說在這麼寒冷的天氣裡，兔子大都待在窩裡不出來。不過她們還是在一些樹木和彎曲的柳樹下，找到幾條紮紮實實結了冰的古老兔徑，上面的痕跡相當凌亂，而且已經結凍了。契日婭將套索的一頭與一根又長又粗的柳樹枝綁在一起，再放到其中一條兔徑上。她用一些柳樹和雲杉的樹枝圍在套索兩側，這樣兔子就會被引導到陷阱裡。兩個老婆婆設置了幾處陷阱，但是她們對抓到兔

子並不抱太大希望。

走回營地的路上，莎聽到有東西從樹梢跑過的細微聲響。她馬上停住不動，也示意她的朋友照做。

兩人拼了命地希望在夜晚的寂靜中再次聽到那個聲音。離她們不遠的一棵樹，在銀色月光下顯現出整個剪影輪廓，她們看到一隻正在探頭探腦的松鼠。莎慢慢把手移到腰帶上，拿起短柄小斧。她盯著那隻松鼠，動作放得非常慢，用小斧對準那個決定她們能否存活的目標。松鼠立刻抬起頭，當莎揮動手臂擲出斧頭的同時，牠迅速往樹上衝。莎

早就預知松鼠會這麼跑，因此刻意把斧頭擲高，結束了這隻小動物的生命。這

一個經過計算的擲斧動作，展現出她已經很久不用的技巧和打獵知識。

契日婭鬆了一大口氣。銀色的月光灑落在莎那張面帶微笑的臉龐，她的聲

音裡帶著驕傲和一些虛弱⋯⋯「我以前做過許多次相同的事，但是我沒想到現在

還會再做一次。」

回到營地之後，她們將松鼠肉放在雪水裡煮熟，喝松鼠肉湯，並且留下一

小部分肉，準備之後再吃。因為她們很清楚，如果把食物吃完，這一餐，也許

就是最後一餐了。

這兩個老婆婆已經有段時間沒有吃東西了，因為部落的人想保存僅剩的一

點食物。現在她們才知道之前沒有分配到食物的原因。為什麼要把食物浪費在

兩個快死的人身上呢？她們試著不去想這些事，低著頭喝松鼠肉湯，把肚子

填飽，然後就到帳篷裡休息，度過這個夜晚。

用來休息的帳篷，是以兩張野牛皮包住三根架成好似三角形的長木頭組合

而成。帳篷裡是堆得厚厚的雲杉樹枝，上面鋪著許多張皮毛毯。她們注意到，

雖然族人讓她們自生自滅，卻還是好心留下所有物品。她們懷疑這是酋長所施的小小恩惠。部落裡低於酋長身分的其他尊貴成員，一定會認為這兩個老婆婆很快就要死了，所以肯定會帶走所有東西，而只留下她們身上穿著的暖和皮毛衣物。這兩個又老又虛弱的老婆婆，就在這些紛亂思緒中打著盹。

月光靜靜灑在這片冰凍的大地上，生命在這塊土地上低語，只有偶然傳來的孤狼悲嚎才會破壞這份寧靜。她們的眼皮因為疲憊憂慮的夢境而不由自主抽動著，雙脣之間發出微微的無助夢囈。當月亮低垂在西邊的地平線，某處傳來劃破夜空的淒厲叫聲。兩個老婆婆立刻驚醒，心裡暗自希望這聲尖叫只是噩夢的一部分。但是哀號聲再次響起。這一次，她們認出這個聲音是來自設置的陷阱所捕捉到的某個動物。深怕其他掠食者會把獵物搶走，她們很快穿好衣服趕到陷阱處。到了那裡，她們看到一隻正在發抖的小兔子，身體有一部分被陷阱綁住，眼神充滿戒備。莎毫不猶豫地走到兔子旁邊，一手伸到牠的脖子上感覺脈搏，接著緊緊捏住，直到這頭不斷掙扎的小動物停止不動。莎將陷阱重新設置好之後，她們一起回到營地，兩個人對未來都多了一絲希望。

早晨的到來並沒有為這片遙遠的北方土地帶來光明。契日婭先醒來。她小心翼翼為火堆添加柴薪，讓原本微弱的火苗變旺。當火堆在寒冷的夜裡逐漸熄滅，她們呼出的溫熱空氣所結成的霜，已經一層層累積在野牛皮搭成的帳篷上。

契日婭對著這單調乏味的陰沉天氣嘆了一口氣後，走到帳篷外，北極星仍然明亮地在天上閃耀著，其他星星也像眨眼似的一閃一閃著。契日婭站了一會兒，看著這些不可思議的星星。她這輩子，對夜晚的星空總是懷抱著一份敬畏之心。

想起還有工作要做，契日婭抓住野牛皮上緣，將野牛皮鋪在地上，熟練地將外層結的霜刷掉。她又走進帳篷裡，把營火生大。濕氣很快化為水珠，從野牛皮上滴下來，然後一下子就乾了。

契日婭驚覺，以前天寒地凍時，這些結霜融化的水滴為什麼沒有掉到她們身上？以前都是怎麼做的？啊，對了！因為年輕人一直都在火堆附近添加柴薪，不時檢查帳篷，確定年長者附近的火堆沒有熄滅。她們以前真是被寵壞了！這樣要如何繼續生存下去呢？

契日婭深深嘆了一口氣，試著不去想那些讓人沮喪的事，而把注意力放在照顧火堆上，盡量不吵醒她正在睡覺的朋友。帳篷裡相當溫暖，火堆發出細微的劈啪聲，乾燥的木頭上，偶爾迸出細小的火花。莎在這種細微的劈啪聲中慢慢醒來，仰躺在地上好長一段時間才注意到契日婭。她慢慢將痠痛的脖子轉過來，微笑著，但是一看到她朋友的孤苦表情，隨即收起笑臉。莎小心地用手肘將自己的身體撐起來，臉上表情痛苦，但仍試著用笑容鼓勵她的朋友，她說：

「當我在妳生起的溫暖火堆旁醒來，還以為昨天只是一場夢。」

契日婭勉強擠出一絲笑容，很明顯是希望讓自己振作起來，但是她還是呆呆地看著火苗。「我只要一坐下來就會開始擔心，」過了很長一段時間後，她說，「我很害怕接下來要面對的事情，不，什麼都別說！」她的朋友已經張開嘴巴準備說話，但她舉起手阻止了。

「我知道妳對於我們能不能生存下去很有信心。妳比較年輕。」她的臉上不禁露出一絲苦笑，因為就在昨天，她們兩個都被認定已經太老了，無法再跟年輕人一起生活。」「我獨自一人生活已經是很久以前的事了，因為身邊一直都有人照顧我，而現在……」她的聲音愈來愈低，眼淚也因為慚愧而流了下來。

她的朋友莎讓她盡情地哭。等到淚水止住，契日婭將自己被眼淚淹沒的臉擦乾後，笑著說：「原諒我，我的朋友，我的年紀比妳大，卻哭得跟個小娃娃似的。」

「我們都像剛出生的娃娃，」莎回應著。比較老的契日婭婆婆聽到她這樣形容，驚訝地抬起頭。「就像沒人幫忙的小娃娃。」莎的雙肩擠出一個笑容。

契日婭看到這個笑容，表情看起來有點受到侮辱。不過在契日婭還沒有誤會她的意思之前，莎繼續說：「我們在這麼長的生命中學到很多東西。但是現在我們都老了，以為已經完成生命中該做的事，所以停下來，並認為原本就該是這樣。我們不再像以前那樣工作，即使我們的身體還很健康，足以擔負比想像中更多的工作。」

契日婭坐著靜靜地聽，警覺到她的朋友就快將事情的真相揭露，那也是為什麼部落裡的年輕人認為拋下她們是最好的選擇。「我們總是抱怨，永遠不會

滿足，老是抱怨沒有食物，老是說以前多好多好，而事實上根本沒那麼好。我們總是認為自己很老了。

現在，由於我們花了很多時間讓年輕人相信我們一點忙也幫不上，因此，他們認為我們對這個世界一點用都沒有。」

莎看到她的朋友聽到最後，眼眶中已經滿是眼淚，便語重心長地繼續說道：「我們要證明他們是錯的！要向部落和死亡證明，他們是錯的！」她搖搖頭，像是要把什麼東西甩到空氣中。「是的，它等著我們，死亡等著我們。它準備在我們示弱的時候，一把抓走我們。我擔心這樣的死亡會遠遠超過我們所經歷的任何痛苦，所以即使我們終將要死，也要奮力一搏！」

契日婭凝視著她的朋友良久，很清楚莎說的一點也沒錯，如果她們不試著求生存，那麼死亡很快就會到來。但令人懷疑的是，她們兩個是不是夠強壯來度過這個嚴酷的冬季。只是莎的聲音中的熱情讓她感覺好多了。所以，她不再覺得悲傷，因為沒有其他選擇。她最後面露微笑說：「我想，我們之前就說過這句話，以後也許還要說很多次，但是，沒錯，讓我們奮力一搏。」她感覺到一股之前覺得不可能出現的力量充滿全身。莎報以微笑，並起身，為這即將到來的漫長一日作準備。

第三章

找回古老的技巧

那一天，她們把時間都花在找回那些年輕時所學到的技巧和知識上。

她們從製作雪鞋開始。通常採集白樺木最好的時節是在晚春和初夏之間，但是今天她們只能將就著選擇幼小的白樺樹。當然，她們並沒有適當的工具，只能利用手邊現有的東西將每根木頭劈成四條，再放到以白樺木製成的大容器裡煮沸。等木條變軟，再把木條彎成半圓，兩端靠齊併攏。然後拿起用來縫紉的錐子，艱難地在兩側木條上鑽出許多小洞。鑽洞的工作雖然非常辛苦，手指雖然疼痛難當，她們仍持續進行直到完成。在此之前，她們已將皮條浸在水裡，現在則把軟化的皮條拿出來撕細，並開始編織雪鞋。

藉著營火的熱度烘烤，當雪鞋的皮條再度變硬時，她們便去準備用來綑紮雪鞋的皮索。

雪鞋做好之後，她們的臉上滿是欣喜的驕傲，穿上那兩雙有點簡陋、卻完全能發揮效用的雪鞋，到雪地裡檢查捕兔陷阱。當她們發現又抓到另外一隻兔子，喜悅自是有增無減。她們知道，幾天前部落裡的人在這個區域完全抓不到兔子，不禁覺得自己的好運背後有著一股神祕力量。回到營地後，她們想到自己付出的努力，心頭上的重擔也減輕了一些。

當天晚上，兩個老婆婆討論接下來的計畫。她們都認為，不應該繼續留在這個部落的秋天營地，因為這裡的動物數量不足以讓她們度過漫長寒冬。即使是這樣寒冷的冬天，其他部落也會遷徙，她們很害怕一些可能出現的敵人會找上門，不希望自己暴露在這種危險下。此外，她們也很怕自己部落的人折返，因為對於部落的信任已經消失殆盡，懼怕這個寒冬會迫使族人們為了求生存而做出殘忍的事。兩個老婆婆決定必須離開這裡，她們沒有忘記那代代流傳下來的禁忌故事——關於人們為了生存而吃人的故事。

　　兩個老婆婆坐在帳篷裡，思考著未來的去處。契日婭突然脫口而出：「我知道一個地方！」

　　「哪裡？」莎詢問的聲音裡掩不住興奮。

　　「妳記不記得很久以前我們釣魚的地方？那條溪流裡的魚多到我們還得建好多貯藏屋好把魚晾乾？」

　　莎想了一下，試圖在記憶裡尋找。她模糊地想到一個地方。「有了，我記得。」

　　但是為什麼後來我們從沒有再回那裡？」她問。

　　契日婭聳聳肩表示她也不知道。

　　「也許部落的人忘了有這個地方的存在。」她小心翼翼地說。

不管是什麼原因，兩人都同意去那兒是個好主意，而且因為距離很遠，所以得立刻動身。她們迫不及待想要盡快離開這個有著傷心回憶的地方。

接下來的早晨，兩個老婆婆開始打包行李。她們的野牛皮可以用在許多地方。這一天，野牛皮的用途就是一個可以拖著走的雪橇。她們把兩張野牛皮從帳篷的支架上拿下來，將有皮毛的一面朝向雪地鋪平後，再把所有物品整齊地排在野牛皮上，最後用長皮條把行李緊緊捆起來。她們又將麋鹿皮革編成的繩子綁在皮毛雪橇前端，再各自把一條繩子綁在手腕上。野牛皮的皮毛在積雪很深的乾燥雪地上能夠輕巧滑動，而她們的雪鞋也讓雪地步行稍微輕鬆一點。兩個老婆婆漫長的旅程就此開始。

溫度變得更低了，冷冽的空氣像針一樣刺痛老婆婆的雙眼。她們不時用裸露的雙手溫暖自己的臉，還得將因眼睛不舒服而流出的淚水擦掉。不過身上的皮毛衣物將她們保護得很好，即使天氣這麼寒冷，身體仍是溫暖的。

她們一直走到夜幕低垂才停下來。雖然沒有走太久，但是兩個人都筋骨痠痛，彷彿走了一輩子的路。她們決定就地露營，在雪地裡挖了幾個深坑，並在裡面填滿雲杉樹枝。接著生起一堆小小的營火，將松鼠肉重新煮過，把湯喝掉。

因為疲累不堪，她們很快就進入夢鄉。只是這次沒有以往的夢魘或是不安的眼皮跳動，她們沉沉地睡著，沒有發出一絲聲音。

清晨來臨，兩個老婆婆在酷寒的環繞中醒來，天頂猶如一個盛著繁星的大碗。但是當她們試著從坑裡爬出來時，身體卻不聽使喚，動也不動。兩個人彼此對望著，心裡明白她們已經讓身體超過所能負擔的限度。最後，比較年輕、也比較有毅力的莎掙扎著爬起來，只是身上的疼痛實在太強烈，她不禁發出一聲痛苦的哀號。契日婭心知同樣的事也會發生在自己身上，只好先靜靜躺了一會兒，累積勇氣，面對即將到來的疼痛。終於她也慢慢地、痛苦地從休息的地方爬出來。她們一跛一跛地在營地附近走著，希望能讓身上僵硬的關節鬆弛一點。

之後她們把剩下的松鼠肉吃完，緩緩拖著沉重的雪橇，繼續旅程。

那天該算是她們所度過最長、最艱難的日子之一。她們麻木地蹣跚而行，因為太過疲勞加上年紀老邁，多次摔倒在雪地裡。雖然幾乎要絕望了，但是她們堅持著，心裡明白自己踏出去的每一步，都讓她們更接近目的地。

若隱若現的日光只出現了一會兒，透過懸浮在空氣中的冰霧看出去，每天都是朦朦朧朧的。

現在，蔚藍的天空再度映入眼簾，但是大多數時候，她們只注意到自己呼出來的那股厚重霧氣在空氣中捲動。肺部凍傷是她們擔心的另一件事，因此一直注意著不要在寒冷中做太辛苦的工作；如果不得不做，她們也會再戴上一層面罩保護自己。但這樣的保護方式會產生一些麻煩，像是結在面罩上的冰霜會不斷摩擦著臉頰，感覺很不舒服。但是，和疼痛的四肢、僵硬的關節，與腫脹的雙腳相較，這種輕微的不適已顯得微不足道。

甚至有時當她們拉動綁在胸前的繩子往前走時，後面沉重的雪橇已不再讓人討厭，因為它可以讓她們免於正面摔倒在雪地上。

當太陽悄悄溜走之後的幾個小時，她們的眼睛會重新適應身邊席捲而至的黑暗。但是她們知道，夜晚其實還沒來臨，還有時間繼續往前走。等到準備停下來紮營歇腳，看見樹木勾勒出的湖岸輪廓，才發現自己正身處在一個大湖邊。她們很清楚，森林才是比較理想的紮營地點，但是兩人實在累壞了，連一步都走不動了。所以她們再一次在雪地裡挖了深坑，舒服地蜷縮在裡面，身上蓋著動物皮革的毯子，很快就睡著了。厚重的動物皮毛外衣將熱氣保持在身體裡，把寒冷的空氣隔絕在外。雪坑和任何一個地面上的帳蓬一樣溫暖，所以她們睡得非常放鬆，完全沒有發覺外頭的溫度冷到足以讓最強悍的北方動物都要找地方避寒。

隔天早晨，莎先醒過來。睡了長長的一覺，加上迎面吹來的寒冷空氣，讓頭腦異常清明。她皺著眉，忍著身上的疼痛，探頭到雪坑外觀察四周，看到樹木生長在湖邊所形成的輪廓，才想起昨天有多麼累，根本沒有辦法跨越這座湖。

她慢慢起身，一方面不想打擾到她的朋友睡覺，另一方面也知道，只要一個動作不對，她那僵硬的身體就會整個鎖死，拒絕再動一下。她回想起幾天前，她和她的朋友還對身上那一點痠痛抱怨連連，嘴角不禁浮出一絲微笑；而這時也才想到，平常走路慣用的枴杖，在前天離開營地時根本忘了帶。在寒風中微微伸展著身體的她，提醒自己要在適當的時候告訴朋友關於枴杖的事。這麼多年來，她們為了走路比較方便，都帶著枴杖，但是現在不知為何，沒有枴杖也走了這麼多哩路。以後兩人聊到這件事，肯定會覺得很好笑。莎穿上雪鞋，準備走走路，好讓因僵硬而疼痛不堪的關節鬆弛一下。

契日婭躺在雪坑裡，抬頭看著她那動作比較敏捷的朋友，緩慢地繞著休息的地方走動。契日婭還是很累，覺得全身都不舒服，但是她知道，一定要盡全力和朋友一同努力度過這個難關。活了這麼久的經驗告訴她，如果放棄了，她的朋友也會跟著放棄，所以契日婭強迫自己起身，但是充斥全身的疼痛讓她又躺了回去，並發出一聲長長的嘆息。

莎看到契日婭辛苦的想爬出來，所以彎下腰想幫契日婭爬出雪坑。她們一起發出吃力的悶哼聲，掙扎著行動。很快地兩人又走在一起，而且一直往前走到湖邊才停下。她們在那裡生了個火堆，小心分配好兔子肉的份量，將肉吃完後才回到雪橇旁，繼續她們的旅程。

冰凍的湖似乎一望無際。她們艱難地穿過許多雲杉、柳樹林，以及生長在湖泊間的一堆帶刺植物，這耗盡了她們的體力，不禁覺得自己比預期的多走了很多路。雖然必須蜿蜒前進才能繞過障礙，她們卻從來沒有失去方向感；雖然有時疲勞會影響她們的判斷，而稍微偏離了前進的路線，或是繞著圈子走，但是她們總能很快找到正確方向。即使不切實際，她們心裡總是不時希望那個找尋中的沼澤會突然出現在眼前。的確，有時候老婆婆也會幻想自己已經到達目的地，但是強勁的寒風和痠痛的骨頭不斷提醒著她們，很快將她們帶回現實。

到了第四天晚上，她們幾乎是跌跌撞撞地在沼澤裡前進。四周聳立的景物都覆蓋了一層銀色月光，樹木的陰影交錯延伸在整個沼澤中。她們在岸邊站著休息一陣子，將那片特別迷人的夜景盡收眼底。莎驚歎著這片土地的力量，它征服了像她這樣生活的人們，征服了動物，甚至連樹木都俯首稱臣。生物全都仰賴這片土地，如果不去遵守這片土地的規則，死亡便會迅雷不及掩耳、不經審判地降臨在粗心大意和沒有生存價值的生命上。莎嘆了一口氣，契日婭看著她的朋友問道：「怎麼了？」

莎的臉上露出苦笑：「沒什麼，我的朋友。我們的確走在正確的小徑上，但心裡想的卻是，我曾經那麼輕鬆如意地生活在這片土地上，而現在這片土地似乎不要我了。也許只是身上的關節痛得很，才讓我抱怨連連。」

契日婭笑了起來：「也許是因為我們的身體實在太老了，或者是我們的狀況不太好，但也許哪一天，我們還是能再一次奔跑，越過這片土地。」莎也跟著開玩笑。

這樣的玩笑話除了讓彼此振奮，沒有別的意義，兩個老婆婆很清楚，旅程尚未結束，掙扎著求生存的過程也不會變得比較容易。雖然她們年紀大了，已經不像從前那麼堅強，但是莎和契日婭明白，在這片土地賜給她們任何溫暖以前，她們還是必須辛勤工作，付出代價。

兩人往下走到強風吹拂的沼澤，直到碰到一條大河。她們知道即使此時天氣嚴寒，河底湍急的水流還是會慢慢融化冰層，使得冰層變薄，行走在冰面上變得相當危險，因此在穿越這條平靜的河流時，她們格外小心，寸步前進，時時留心冰面裂開的聲音，或是狹窄的冰縫間有沒有蒸汽冒出來等徵兆。

終於抵達河流對岸，壓力和勞累使得兩個老婆婆身心俱疲。她們用僅剩的一點氣力，開始動手搭起另一個過夜用的帳篷。

第四章

痛苦的旅程

當她們準備搭帳篷過夜，才發現之前的夜晚沒有一個能比得上今晚，因為她們實在太累了，幾乎連動都動不了。她們盲目的、搖搖晃晃地搜集用來鋪床的雲杉樹枝，和生營火用的大木頭。最後回到原地，用從上個營地帶來、尚未熄滅的煤炭生起了營火。她們頭腦混沌地凝視著火堆裡的大片橙色焰火，一下子就昏昏沉沉地睡著了，完全沒有聽見遠處狼隻孤寂的嚎叫。等聽到狼叫聲時，早晨的冰冷空氣已讓她們恢復知覺。

兩個老婆婆睡著的時候，互相靠在一起。不知為何，兩人一整晚都維持著盤腿而坐的姿勢不動。她們知道要起身肯定不容易，因而靜靜地坐了很長一段時間。莎率先試著站起來，但是腿已經失去了知覺。她悶哼著再試一次。這時，契日婭緊閉著眼睛，假裝還在睡。她一點都不想面對今天。

莎鼓起一絲勇氣逼自己動一動，但是骨頭深處的疼痛感如此劇烈，她知道這次一定站不起來。她們又再一次讓自己的身體超過能負荷的限度。莎不由自主發出一聲痛苦的吶喊，感受到一股想大哭一場的強烈衝動。她抱著頭，想到這些日子以來所經歷的一切，覺得自己完全被擊潰了，而四周的寒冷讓她更加絕望。不管怎麼努力，身體就是不肯動一下。她全身四肢實在太僵硬了。

契日婭不動聲色，聽著朋友嗚咽。她很驚訝自己居然能夠坐著聽莎的哭聲，心裡卻不為所動。也許她們再繼續走下去也沒什麼意義，也許那些年輕人是對的，她和莎對抗的是一件無法避免的事。對她們來說，鑽進溫暖的皮衣沉沉睡去應該比較容易，再也不用向任何人證明什麼。也許莎所害怕的長眠沒有那麼糟糕，至少不會像這樣動彈不得那麼糟。

雖然莎現在的意志力和契日婭一樣脆弱，但她卻在此時展現一股堅強的決心。無視於寒冷、身上的疼痛、空空的胃和麻木的腿，她奮力站起，而這一次她成功了。就如同早上起床的習慣，她繞著營火一跛一跛地走著，直到感覺血管裡的血液慢慢在流動。當感覺恢復之後，疼痛變得更加劇烈，莎索性將全部注意力轉移到搜集生火用的木頭上，然後煮一鍋美味的兔子頭湯。

契日婭瞇著眼睛看著這一切，不希望朋友知道她已經醒了。一會兒後，雖然覺得自己有義務起身動一動，然而她卻完全不想動，一丁點兒也不想。她只希望維持現在的姿勢，也許死亡很快就會偷偷把她從痛苦中帶走。但身體似乎還沒準備好要交給死神，因而不如預期般快樂地睡著，只覺一陣強烈的尿意來襲，催促著她去解放膀胱的壓力。她試著不去管那股尿意，但是膀胱再也等不及了。她大喊一聲後，感到膀胱一陣鬆，心一急，跳起來朝柳樹直衝過去，也嚇了她的朋友一大跳。等契日婭從柳樹後面走出來，臉上帶著微微的罪惡表情。莎一臉疑惑，歪著頭：「出了什麼問題嗎？」契日婭很尷尬地說：「從不知道我可以跑得這麼快，我以為自己再也動不了了。」

「我們走出的每一步，都會讓我們離目的地更近一點。雖然今天走，」她說，「我們吃飽之後，應該試著繼續往前莎思索著接下來的一天要怎麼過。

覺得不舒服，但我的意志力比我的身體知覺還要強大，它要我們繼續往前走，而不是待在這裡休息，即使我也想休息。」契日婭一面喝著兔子頭湯，一面聽莎說話。契日婭雖然想在這裡停留一會兒，事實上，她非常希望留下來，但是覺得很羞愧，只好拋開那個愚蠢的想法，不情願地同意她們應該繼續走下去。

聽到契日婭同意繼續這段旅程，莎微微感到失望。她心想，在自己的內心深處是希望契日婭拒絕的，但是現在想這個已經太晚了。她們倆把繩子綁在瘦弱的手腕上，開始拉著雪橇往前行。老婆婆一面走，一面留心動物出沒的痕跡，因為食物已經快吃完了，而肉是主要的能量來源。沒有了食物，很快就會喪失求生鬥志。她們偶爾會停下來討論所選的路線，並問自己走的路對不對。不過河流從沼澤分出之後只流往一個方向，所以只要沿著河岸走，並注意尋找一條狹窄的小溪，那條小溪就會帶領她們抵達那個久遠記憶中有很多魚群的地方。

日子在她們緩緩拖動雪橇、穿越深深積雪中過去。到了第六天，莎呆呆望著前方的路，碰巧抬起頭，看看四周，看到河的對岸開了一個口，連接著一條小溪。「我們到了。」她用軟綿綿、有氣無力的聲音說。契日婭看看她的朋友，再看看那條小溪：「只是我們是在錯的這一邊。」她說。莎擠出一絲微笑，她的朋友似乎總是看到事情的黑暗面，但她已經累得沒法拋出些正面的想法，莎對自己嘆了一口氣，示意她的朋友跟上來。

這一次，兩個老婆婆不再擔心冰面下是不是藏著什麼裂縫。她們實在太累了，無視危險，跨越了結冰的河流，並立刻朝著小溪的上游前進，一直走到夜色已深才停下來。月亮從樹梢慢慢冒出頭來，直到高掛樹尖，照亮這條狹窄小溪旁的路。雖然和前幾天比起來已經多走了好幾個小時，但是兩人仍然繼續走著。她們確定那個古老的營地一定在附近，希望今天晚上就能到達目的地。

就在契日婭準備求她的朋友停下腳步時，她看到了那片營地。「看看那裡啊！」她大喊，「那裡還有好久以前我們掛著的魚架！」莎停下來，突然覺得一陣虛弱，得用很大的力氣才能讓發抖的雙腳站著。一種回家的感覺完全淹沒了她。

契日婭向她的朋友靠近了些，輕輕伸出一隻手臂抱著她。兩個老婆婆互相注視，感到一股無法言語的激動情緒。她們完全靠自己的力量走到這裡。過去

在這裡與朋友、家人共享歡笑的美好回憶，紛紛湧入腦中；現在因為一段醜陋的命運轉折，她們孤零零的待在這裡，而背叛她們的，正是相同的那一群人。

因為一同度過這艱困的時光，兩個老婆婆之間發展出一種默契，她們可以知道對方正在想什麼。在這方面，莎的感覺更為敏銳。

「最好不要去想為什麼我們會在這裡，」她說，「我們必須把今天過夜用的帳篷架起來，明天再聊。」契日婭清了清從喉頭湧上來的一陣苦澀，衷心同意莎的話。所以她們拖著疲累的步伐，爬上小溪旁較低的岸邊，走向那片營地。那裡還有她們以前搭帳篷的支架。

雖然衣服可以保護她們不受惱人的寒冷侵襲，但是野牛皮的禦寒效果更好。火堆裡燃燒的煤炭在灰燼中舞動了一整個晚上，讓整個帳篷暖烘烘的。終於，清晨的寒意偷偷溜進帳篷，她們也開始慢慢被喚醒。第一個準備起身的是莎，這一次身體沒有抗議得太厲害，就能起身在帳篷附近走動，將前一晚搜集到的柴薪放到火堆中尚未完全熄滅的木頭上。她對著乾燥的木頭輕輕吹了一會兒氣，火苗跳著溫柔的舞蹈，慢慢在一捆乾柳樹枝上蔓延開來。帳篷裡一下子就變得既溫暖又明亮。

那一天，她們無視疼痛的關節，持續工作著。她們很清楚，必須趕緊做好最後的準備工作，好面對即將到來更為寒冷的天氣，以度過整個冬天裡最嚴酷的時期。所以她們花了一整天，把雪高高地堆在帳篷四周，用來隔離寒風，並搜集所有可以找到的散落樹枝。她們沒有休息，緊接著設下一長串的捕兔陷阱，因為這裡的柳樹長得相當茂盛，她們發現許多兔子活動的痕跡。等到兩人走回營地，夜晚已經來臨。莎將僅剩的一些兔子內臟煮了，好好享用最後剩下的食物。吃飽後，她們背靠著床邊，凝視著營火。

在被部落拋棄前，兩個老婆婆彼此並不熟識。她們一直是鄰居，同樣有著喜歡抱怨的壞習慣，彼此交談的內容都是一些無關緊要的事。現在兩人的共通點，則是年老和悲慘的命運。所以，就在這個晚上，在這段痛苦旅程的終點，她們反而不知道如何以同伴的身分交談，只是各自沉浸在思緒中。

契日婭的心思立刻飄到她的女兒和孫子身上，想知道他們是否一切平安。

當她再想到自己的女兒，一陣心痛的感覺油然而生。對契日婭來說，實在很難相信親生骨肉會拒絕挺身出來幫助自己。自憐的情緒讓她悲慟不已，她的嘴唇抿成一條細長而堅決的線，強忍著滿滿的淚水。她不會哭！現在是堅強和遺忘的時刻！但即使這樣想，她還是落下一大滴淚。轉頭看著莎，發現她也深深陷在自己的思緒中。契日婭被她的朋友弄得有些困惑。除了某些時候流露出來的脆弱，這個坐在她身旁的老朋友似乎總是堅強而有自信，彷彿生來就是要面對這一切挑戰。好奇心取代了身上的疼痛，契日婭打破沉默開口說話，莎被嚇了一大跳。

「當我還是個小女孩時，他們拋棄了我的祖母。她那時已無法走路，也幾乎失明了。我們是那麼飢餓，每個人走起路來都搖搖晃晃的。我媽媽悄悄說，她很怕大家想吃人。我以前從來沒聽過這種事，但是我的家族流傳著某個人因為太過絕望，而做出這類事情的故事。我緊抓著母親的手，心中滿是恐懼，害怕到如果有人注視我的眼睛，我會很快別過頭去，深怕他注意到我，想把我吃了。那時我的肚子也很餓，不過不知什麼緣故，那對我來說似乎不是很重要。也許是因為年紀太小，只要有家人陪在身邊就好。但當他們說要丟下祖母時，我嚇壞了。我記得我的父親和兄弟們不斷和部落裡的人爭吵，但是當父親回到帳篷時，從他臉上的表情，我明白發生了什麼事；再望向祖母，她已經瞎了，耳朵也聾得聽不見即將發生在自己身上的事。」契日婭深深吸了一口氣，繼續她的故事。

「當他們為她穿好保暖的衣服，並將毯子放在她身邊，我想祖母已經感覺到即將發生的事，因為當我們準備離開營地時，我聽見了她的哭聲。」契日婭發著抖，述說自己的回憶。

「等到長大，我才知道我的兄弟和父親曾掉頭回去，結束了祖母的生命，因為他們不希望她受這種苦。而且他們還將祖母的屍體燒了，以防有人會想以她的肉果腹。最後，我們不知道用了什麼方法度過那個冬天。我記得其他餓著肚子過的冬天，但是沒有一個像那次那麼慘。」

莎哀傷地微笑著，她能體會朋友的那段痛苦記憶。她也說起自己的回憶：

「當我還小的時候，我像個小男孩，」她娓娓道來，「總是和我的兄弟在一起，從他們身上學到很多事。有時候，媽媽會試著要我靜靜坐著縫補衣物，或是學習一些成為女人之後該知道的事情。但是爸爸和兄弟總會救我出去，他們喜歡我原來的樣子。」她微笑地回想著。

「我們家族跟大部分的家族不同。我父親和母親幾乎讓我們做所有的事，會先像別人一樣做一些家庭雜務，但等到事情做完，我們還會到處探險。我從來沒有和其他的小孩玩過，我的玩伴只有兄弟們。我很害怕長大後不知會變成什麼樣子，因為當時的生活是那麼有趣。當媽媽問我是不是已經成為一個女人，我不懂她的意思，以為她說的是年紀，而不是『那一方面』的事。每過一個夏天，她就會問我相同的問題，而她眼中的擔憂也一次次加深。本來我並不是很在意她的反應；但是當我長得和媽媽一樣高、只比我的兄弟矮一點時，人們開始用異樣眼光看著我。比我年輕的女孩都已經有了男人和小孩，但我還是像個孩子一樣自由自在。」莎開懷大笑，因為她現在知道，為什麼當時每個人看著她的表情，都是一臉詫異。

「我開始聽到他們在背後譏笑我，我不明所以。在某種程度上，我並不在意別人怎麼看我，所以繼續打獵、釣魚、探險，做自己喜歡的事。媽媽試圖讓我待在家工作，但我堅決不肯。我的兄弟已經找到女人，我告訴媽媽那個女人可以幫很多忙，這樣我就能逃開。當我媽要求爸爸要好好管教我，我就會拿出一大堆鴨子、魚和其他食物，而我的父親就只是說：『別管她了。』後來我的年紀愈來愈大，已經超過該有男人和小孩的年紀，每一個人都在說我的事情。

我不懂為什麼，因為即使沒有找到男人，沒有生小孩，我還是將我該做的供給食物的工作做好。有段時間，我帶回來的食物甚至比男人還多，但他們並未因此特別高興。就在此時，我們碰上最糟糕的一個冬天，就像這次冬天那麼冷。」

莎揮動著手。

「連嬰兒都活不成，成年男人開始緊張，因為他們已經竭盡全力，仍然找不到足夠的動物果腹。酋長決定要繼續前進以尋找食物，那時候大家都謠傳很遠的地方可以找到野牛，這個謠言讓每個人都興奮莫名。

「在我們這個族群裡，有一個我鮮少注意到的老婆婆，必須倚賴別人拖著她走。酋長不想要這個負擔，所以告訴大家把她留下。沒有人抗議，除了我以外。我的母親試著阻止我抗議，告訴我這麼做是為了整個部落的人好。就像一個冷漠沒有感情的陌生人，我氣得把她撥到一旁。不過，年紀輕輕的我並沒有想太多，除了很震驚，也很混亂。我覺得部落的人一直都很懶惰，沒有好好把事情想清楚，而我的工作就是要讓他們恢復理智。本著自己的良知，我挺身而出，為那個幾乎才剛剛認識的老婆婆說話。我逼問族人，是否覺得自己比那些躲開虛弱老狼的狼群好？

「那個酋長是個殘忍的人。我一直都避著他，直到那天我站在他的面前，正對著他，憤怒地大吼。看得出來，他的憤怒比我還強兩倍，但是我沒辦法不把話說出來。即使知道酋長不喜歡我，我還是不聽他的話，努力爭辯，而他也試著回答我提出的控訴。他的做法是錯的，我一心想要糾正他。當我說話的同時，我沒有注意到自己帶給部落的人什麼樣的震撼，他們彷彿從飢餓的昏沉中醒了過來。酋長臉上露出害怕的神色，伸出他的大手遮住了我的嘴巴⋯⋯『好吧，奇怪的年輕女孩。』他說話的聲音很大，我很清楚那是為了羞辱我。我可以感覺我的下巴抬得更高，這樣他就能清楚看到我臉上的驕傲和勇敢。『妳留下來和那個老婆婆作伴。』他說。我聽到母親深深吸了一口氣，而我自己的心直往下沉。但我還是不肯退讓，眼睛眨也不眨，直直地看著他的眼睛。

「我的家族受到很深的傷害，但是驕傲和恥辱讓他們沒有出聲抗議，他們不希望有個女兒和部落裡強而有力的領袖發生這麼大的衝突。我並不覺得那些領導者比較厲害。在那之後，酋長好像當我不存在一樣；除了家族的人，每個人都假裝我不存在。我的家人一直求我去向酋長道歉，但是我不肯妥協。每當有人假裝我不存在，我的驕傲就多了一分，而且我還一直為那個老婆婆請命。」莎想到自己那段衝動的年輕歲月，不禁笑出聲來。

「接下來怎麼樣了？」契日婭很好奇。

莎停頓了一下，深深吸了一口來自遙遠記憶的痛苦。她用一種強作鎮定的聲音說：「他們走了之後，我就沒有那麼勇敢了。方圓幾哩之內根本找不到動物，但是我決定要讓他們看看，在我的努力下，我們可以做到什麼地步。所以那個老婆婆和我吃老鼠、吃貓頭鷹，任何會跑的我們都吃。我把動物殺了，然後兩個人一起吃掉。我一直都不知道那個老婆婆的名字，因為我一直忙著讓我們倆活下去。那個老婆婆沒能活過那個冬天，最後只剩我一個人，我的驕傲和平常的無憂無慮這時都幫不上忙。我一直自言自語：『有沒有人在？』如果部落的人回來看到我對著空氣說話，一定會認為我瘋了。至少你和我還有彼此可以說說話。」莎對她的朋友說，而契日婭衷心點點頭。

「此後我才了解到，跟著一大群人的重要性。身體需要食物，心靈卻需要人群。當陽光長時間散發熱力照耀大地時，我開始探索這片荒野。有一天我獨自走著，像平常一樣自言自語，忽然有人回應：『妳在跟誰說話？』那一瞬間，我以為自己聽到什麼而止步，慢慢轉過身去，發現有個看起來很強壯高大的男人，雙手抱胸，很有自信地對著我微笑。那時我的心裡滿是複雜的感受，驚訝、尷尬、生氣的情緒一股腦兒全都冒出來。『你嚇了我一大跳！』我說，試圖隱藏我真正的感覺；但因為我的臉頰紅得發燙，還有在他笑得更開心的臉上，我知道沒能騙過他。他問我一個人在那裡做什麼，我就把故事全告訴他。那時，我覺得他是一個可以信任的人。他告訴我，相同的事也發生在他身上，只不過他被趕出部落的原因是，他笨到去搶一個心已另有所屬的女人。後來我們在一起很長一段時間之後，才變成一個女人和一個男人的關係。之後我再也沒有見到家人，好幾年後我們才加入部落。」

「最後他因為試著和一頭熊打架而死了，笨男人。」她怨懟的語氣中帶著讚賞，臉上則是深沉的哀傷。

那是契日婭第一次看到她的朋友這麼哀傷，她打破沉默說：「妳比我幸運多了，因為當我明顯對於和男人共同生活沒有什麼興趣時，卻被逼著跟一個比我老很多的男人住在一起，可以說我根本不認識他。過了好幾年我們才有了小孩，他去世的時候比我現在還老。」

莎笑了起來。「部落的人本來也準備幫我選一個男人，如果我跟他們待在一起的時間再久一點的話。」沉默了一下子，她繼續說，「現在看看我們，老得連骨頭喀啦喀啦響都聽得見，而且還被丟下來自生自滅。」她們又陷入沉默，腦袋裡各自糾結著不同的情緒。她們躺到溫暖的床上，任由外頭寒冷的大地發抖哆嗦。兩個老婆婆想著剛剛分享的經驗，在累得沉沉睡去之前，覺得此時此地，家的感覺更濃厚了，因為對於彼此的認識更深，也因為她們都曾在艱困中活過來。

太陽落入地平線的地方一天比一天低，白晝的時間愈來愈短。天氣變得更冷，有幾次周遭樹木甚至因寒冷的壓力而爆裂，發出的巨大聲響讓她們嚇得跳起來；連柳樹都因為太冷而斷裂。當一切安置妥當，她們除了開始擔心遠處嚎叫的凶猛狼群，其他想像出來的恐懼也不斷折磨著她們；漫漫長夜，有的是時間讓她們胡思亂想。她們利用僅剩不多的白晝強迫自己到處走動，所有走路的時間都用來搜集埋在深雪下的柴火。雖然食物短缺，但保持溫暖更要緊。到了晚上，她們會坐下來聊天，試著讓彼此遠離寂寞和恐懼的陰影。部落裡的人很少將寶貴的時間花在無意義的聊天上，說話的時候多半是在溝通，而不是社交。但是這兩個老婆婆在這些漫長的夜晚中打破了慣例，她們聊天，且隨著更加了解對方過去的艱困體驗，進而發展出相互尊重的感覺。

抓到更多兔子是很久之後的事，那時她們已經好幾天沒有好好吃一頓了。她們本來準備把雲杉樹枝放在水裡煮，當薄荷茶喝，以保存體力，不過這卻讓胃變得更酸。她們知道經過這段有一餐沒一餐的日子，貿然吃下固體食物會是一種危險的舉動，所以先將兔子肉煮成一鍋營養的湯，慢慢喝下去。喝了一天

的湯之後，她們才小心吃一片兔子肉；再經過幾天，才增加食物中肉的分量。

很快地，兩人的體力就完全恢復了。

帳蓬旁的木頭已經堆得像柵欄一樣高，她們這才花更多時間去尋找食物。

年輕時學到的狩獵技巧，這時又再度派上用場。每一天，她們都會走到離帳篷更遠的地方去架設兔子陷阱，並注意有沒有其他小動物可以捕獵。她們學到的其中一條規則是，如果你設下捕捉動物的陷阱，就必須定時查看，而不必理會陷阱皮條是否會帶來霉運。所以，即使天氣寒冷或身體不舒服，她們每天都還是會去檢查陷阱，而且通常會有一隻兔子作為他們的獎勵。

等到夜幕低垂，日間工作告一段落，她們會把兔子皮毛編成毯子、手套、面罩等衣物。偶爾為了讓工作不那麼單調，她們會互相拿出一頂用兔子皮毛編織的帽子或是手套給對方看，而這總是讓兩人開懷不已。

隨著日子一天天過去，天氣也不像之前那麼嚴酷，兩個老婆婆終於能夠享受快樂時光，因為她們已經度過這個冬天！恢復體力的兩人，現在忙著搜集更多柴火、檢查兔子陷阱，並且搜索這一大片區域，看看有沒有其他動物。雖然兩個老婆婆已經沒有抱怨的習慣，但是對於每天吃兔子肉已感到厭煩，她們想吃一些別的肉，像是柳樹松雞、樹松鼠和河狸。

有天早上，契日婭醒來後，覺得有什麼事情很不對勁。她慢慢起身，心臟卻怦怦跳得很快。她擔心是不是最糟糕的事情要發生了，一面偷看帳篷外的情形。一開始，一切看起來跟以前沒什麼兩樣，接著突然看到一群柳樹松雞正在啄附近一些樹枝碎片。她的手顫抖著，靜靜從編織袋裡拿出一根又長又細的皮條，慢慢地爬到帳篷外，又從身旁的木頭堆裡，挑了一根細長的木棍，在木棍

尾端做了一個套索，開始爬向那群松雞。

松雞注意到老婆婆出現，緊張地咕咕叫了起來。契日婭知道這些鳥已經準備要跟她打架了。

她停了幾分鐘，讓牠們有時間冷靜下來。松雞現在離她並不遠，希望莎不要在這個時候醒來發出聲響，把這群雞嚇跑。契日婭忍著膝蓋的疼痛，伸出微微發抖的手，慢慢將木棍伸出去。幾隻松雞緊張地飛到附近松樹上，但是她不為所動，繼續將木棍伸向其他沒有飛走，但愈跑愈快的松雞。契日婭把注意力放在離自己最近的一隻松雞上，牠朝著套索走近了一些，頭前前後後點著。

就在這隻雞發出聒噪的叫聲，邊跑邊準備飛起的那一刻，契日婭將套索丟出去，不偏不倚落在松雞頭上。她拿著木棍用力向上一扯，那隻雞一面翻滾，一面發出淒厲的叫聲，最後終於動也不動。契日婭站起身，手上提著死掉的松雞回到帳篷時，她的朋友臉上滿是笑意，她也報以微笑。

契日婭吸了一口氣，發現空氣裡帶著一股溫暖。「天氣愈來愈好了。」莎輕輕地說。契日婭很驚訝，眼睛張得老大：「我早該注意到的。如果天氣還很冷的話，我的姿勢大概會凍成一隻偷偷摸摸的狐狸。」她們一面大笑，一面走回帳篷，準備處理這個來自不同季節的肉食。那天早上之後，天氣在苦寒與帶點溫暖的下雪日之間轉換。她們沒有再抓到另外一隻鳥，口腹之慾雖然沒有得到紓解，但此時白天已經慢慢變得更長、更溫暖，也更明亮。

Ts'it Han (Porcupine River)

Tr'aanjik

Nahtryaa Van

Ditsik ehdlii ddhah

Chahalie Van

K'ahdaii

Njuu Tsal Van

Tsuk Van

J.L.Grant
©23

Trahkyaa Zhrah Van

Chtaatritt Van

Njuu Choh Van

Jokoei Van

Ohtg Van

ARCTIC CIRCLE

Tt'oochyaa Kat
(Grass River)

Vunlau Van

這份路線圖是用一般的育空平原地圖畫出來的，繪製過程得到我母親很多協助。冬季小徑在細節上未必和歷史紀錄完全吻合，但也確實顯示了西方文明到來之前，哥威迅人長期活動的大致區域。哥威迅人使用了許多冬季和夏季小徑，但是經過了這麼多年，這些小徑若不是已經被人遺忘，就是被尋求捷徑的年輕一代或大自然改變了走向。

第五章

貯藏魚乾

冬天很快過去了，兩個老婆婆把更多時間花在狩獵遊戲上。不管是在樹林間活蹦亂跳的小松鼠，或是似乎遍地亂跑的柳樹松雞，都成了她們的盤中佳餚。

春天暖和的日子來臨，就表示獵捕麝鼠的時節到了。很久以前，她們就學會獵捕麝鼠所需的技巧和耐心。首先必須製作特殊的網子和陷阱。將一根柳樹枝彎成半圓形，樹枝兩端牢牢固定，再用麋鹿皮製成的細皮條在柳枝框裡編織，直到編出一個粗陋但堅固的網子。在一個陽光普照的日子，她們出發尋找麝鼠的地道。

她們走了很遠，來到一個大小湖泊群聚的地方，這裡有麝鼠活動的痕跡。她們發現其中一座湖，在融化的冰上可以看到小小的黑色麝鼠窩突起。確定麝鼠地道位置後，她們用一根根的木棍在地道兩頭出口做記號。只要木棍一動，就代表有麝鼠從地道出來；等到麝鼠出了洞口，其中一人會用網子抓住牠，再奮力猛敲一下頭顱，一口氣結束牠的性命。第一天她們就抓到十隻麝鼠。不過由於長時間維持彎腰等待的姿勢，兩人疲憊不堪，走回營地的路似乎也變得更遠了。

春天，她們沒有什麼時間說話或是回想過去，兩個老婆婆忙著捕捉更多的麝鼠和水獺，這些都是要燻製乾燥之後保存起來的。她們白天忙得幾乎沒有時間吃東西，晚上則累得呼呼大睡。當她們覺得抓到的麝鼠和水獺已經足夠，才將所有東西打包妥當，拖回主營地。

不過，她們覺得這樣還是很不保險。因為現在這個地方的動物很多，到時候其他人也許會回到這裡。通常她們說的「其他人」，是指自己部落的人。自從在寒冷的冬天被拋棄後，她們知道沒有辦法和年輕一代抗衡，而且也很清楚自己對那些人的信任已經消失殆盡了。現在，多疑的心理讓她們擔心，萬一有人來這裡遇見她們，並發現她們的存糧漸漸變多時，會發生什麼事。兩人討論

　了一下，一致應該要趕緊把營地遷
移到比較沒有人想去的地方，或者別人
不會想探索的地方，也許是有著一大群
難以應付的夏天昆蟲之處。

　兩個老婆婆其實一點都不想面對那
些等在濃密柳樹叢或樹林間的嗜血蚊
子，但是她們害怕人更甚於蚊子，於是
打包所有東西，開始艱苦跋涉，前往躲
藏的地點。她們決定在高溫的白天工
作，那時蚊子似乎都躲得不見蹤影；到
了晚上，則坐在冒煙的火堆旁保護自己
不受叮咬。遷徙營地的準備工作花了好
幾天時間，最後，她們站在溪邊，最後
一次環顧這個地方，心裡希望吹起一陣

風，能把她們曾經待在這裡的任何痕跡都吹得無影無蹤。

在決定遷移營地之前，兩個老婆婆曾從樹幹上撕下許多白樺樹皮。現在她們才發現犯了大錯。雖然她們總是相隔很遠一段距離才會再剝下一棵樹木的樹皮，但是任何一個眼尖的人都會注意到這一點。不過，她們也知道已經沒有什麼補救的方法，因此做好心理準備後，便帶著一大捆樹皮離開營地，前往那個不得不去的地方。

在春天剩下的日子裡，兩個老婆婆想辦法將新的營地變得更適合居住。她們將帳篷隱藏在許多柳樹後面，架在一群高大的雲杉樹蔭下。接著找到一個比較陰涼的地方，挖了個很深的洞，裡面鋪上柳樹枝，把夏天要吃的大批肉乾放在洞裡。她們還在洞口附近的地面上設下陷阱，用來嚇跑那些鼻子很靈的肉食動物。這裡到處都是蚊子，工作時，她們靠著很久以前就已使用過的方法，保護自己不致成為蚊子的美食。例如，把皮製的流蘇穗子掛在臉上，再穿上厚厚的衣服，讓小昆蟲叮咬不到；被蚊子騷擾得快抓狂時，她們還會在臉上塗抹麝鼠油，逼退那一大群飛行昆蟲。這段期間，她們還闢了一條通往溪邊的隱密小徑以便取水；為了即將來臨的夏天，也在溪邊設置捕魚的陷阱。當陷阱設置妥當後，她們發現捕魚相當容易，一點都不成問題，因此不得不選擇在靠近溪邊的地方，處理剖魚、乾燥等工作。過了一段時間，有一頭不請自來的熊，肆無忌憚地吃起貯藏的魚。兩個老婆婆非常擔心，但是過了不久，她們和熊似乎達成一項心照不宣的協議：她們把魚的內臟放在離營地很遠的地方，而熊則在那裡自由活動，放心地大快朵頤。

時間流逝得飛快，傍晚的太陽在地平線上已經變成橙色，天氣也涼爽多了，兩個老婆婆很清楚夏天已經所剩無幾。大約就在這個時候，回來產卵的鮭魚開始沿著這條小溪向上游。這對她們來說是天大的好消息，因此有一小段時間，她們一直忙著處理紅通通的魚肉。此時這個區域已經不見熊的蹤影，但她們還是把內臟丟在溪邊。如果熊沒有吃掉那些內臟，偶爾出現的烏鴉也會很快來飽食一頓。兩個老婆婆也很節儉，她們會保留許多魚的器官作其他用途，例如鮭魚的腸子可以用來裝水，而魚皮可以製成圓形的袋子裝魚乾。這些工作讓她們忙得團團轉，得一大清早就起床，直到深夜才能休息。北極的夏天，就在不知不覺中結束了，秋天悄悄來到兩個老婆婆身邊。

在季節變換時，兩個老婆婆結束溪邊捕魚的工作，並把大批處理好的魚拖回祕密營地。接著她們發現一個新的問題：捕到的魚實在太多了，根本沒有地方可以儲存，而且隨著冬天愈來愈近，為了準備過冬而覓食的小動物有增無減。最後她們製作直立式的貯藏架來存放魚，而且在下面放了許多有刺的植物和灌木，希望能讓動物知難而退，打消吃魚的念頭。也許是這個方法真的有用，也可能只是運氣好，動物都沒有靠近她們的貯藏架。

在營地後面很遠的地方有座小山丘，她們一直沒有時間過去看看。由於夏天的打獵工作已經告一段落，有一天，莎一時興起，想知道山丘附近有些什麼，就拿起自己做的矛和弓箭，大聲嚷嚷要到山丘那裡看看。契日婭雖不同意，但是她可以看出她朋友的心意已定。

「只要保持火堆不熄滅，再把矛放在身邊，妳應該就很安全。」莎出發的時候這麼說著，留下身後搖頭不表同意的契日婭。

這是莎獨處的一天。印象中這麼多年來，第一次覺得心頭不像從前那麼緊繃，她像個小孩一樣，貪婪地呼吸著這種感覺。今天天氣好極了，樹葉逐漸轉成明亮的金色，空氣乾爽清新。莎幾乎是蹦跳著走在一條獸徑上。從遠處完全看不出莎是個老婆婆，因為她看起來腳步輕盈，充滿活力。抵達山頂時，她驚訝得倒吸了一口氣：眼前長滿一大片蔓越莓。莎跪在地上一把把摘著這些紅色果實，同時也不忘塞一些在嘴裡。當她正享受著美味食物時，附近灌木叢動了一下，她嚇得立刻靜止不動。

莎一面逼自己慢慢轉頭，望向發出聲音的方向，一面想像最糟的情況。當她發現只是一頭公麋鹿時，著實鬆了一大口氣。接著她才想到，每年這個季節，一頭公麋鹿可能是最讓人畏懼的四腳動物。平常的牠相當羞怯，但是一處於交配季節，就會變得不怕人類，不怕任何在前方移動或擋住牠的東西。

這頭麋鹿靜靜站了很久，彷彿和老婆婆一樣嚇呆了，不知道站在面前的這個人要做什麼。隨著心跳慢慢回復正常，莎想起以前在漫漫冬日中所嘗過的麋鹿肉是何等美味。滿腦袋一陣狂熱、幾近無法思考，她伸手從背包裡抽出一支箭搭在弓上。麋鹿的耳朵朝著她動作的方向翻了一下，接著一轉身，朝反方向

奔馳。莎射出去的箭落在軟地上，沒有造成任何傷害。

莎沒有考慮後果便追了上去。雖然沒辦法跑得像年輕時那麼快，遠遠看起來比較像是一跛一跛地走，而不是在跑步，不過她還是能追在麋鹿後面。麋鹿在任何時候都跑得比人類快，當然積雪很深的時候例外。但今天這種沒有下雪的日子，那頭麋鹿只要一衝，就能把莎遠遠拋在身後，莎大概只能氣喘吁吁地追著，甚至連消失在灌木叢後面的麋鹿大屁股都看不到。但這隻大麋鹿停下來很多次，似乎像是在和莎玩遊戲，每當莎快要追上，牠就會慢條斯理地跑到更遠處。一般來說，麋鹿碰到獵食者都會盡可能跑得遠遠的，但是今天這頭麋鹿似乎不是很想跑，也沒有受到威脅的感覺，所以莎才能一直讓牠保持在視線內。雖然莎很清楚，以她的能力，很難捕捉到這頭麋鹿，但是她很固執，不肯輕易放棄。等到午後稍晚，這頭麋鹿似乎厭倦了這個遊戲，用那對又黑又圓的眼睛斜斜看了莎一眼，耳朵一翻，開始愈跑愈快。到這個時候，莎不得不承認自己根本拿牠沒轍。她喪氣地看著空無一物的灌木叢，慢慢轉身，思忖著：

「如果我再年輕四十歲，也許就能抓到牠了。」

當莎回到營地時，夜已經深了，她的朋友坐在熊熊營火旁警戒著。當莎疲累地坐在一堆雲杉樹枝上，契日婭忍不住脫口而出：「我擔心妳的這段時間，真是度日如年啊！」雖然她的聲音裡帶著不滿，但是能夠看到朋友安然無恙地歸來，契日婭真的鬆了一口氣。

莎知道自己做了傻事，想到她的朋友在這段時間裡的忐忑不安，她又羞又愧。契日婭端來一碗暖暖的魚湯，莎接過後慢慢喝完，等到恢復一些力氣，才把自己這一天的經歷告訴契日婭。想像莎追逐那頭麋鹿的樣子，契日婭不禁笑了出來，不過她的笑容只是淡淡的，因為嘲笑別人並非她的本性。莎很感激契日婭這一點，接著才想到那些蔓越莓，便把這個大發現告訴契日婭，兩人為此興奮不已。

莎花了好幾天時間，才從麋鹿冒險之旅的激動情緒中慢慢回復平靜。這段時間她們安靜地坐著，將白樺樹皮編成一個大圓碗，才又回到山丘上採蔓越莓，而且盡可能多採一點。那時已經入秋，夜晚變得愈來愈冷，似乎提醒著兩個老婆婆別再浪費時間，得趕緊搜集冬天要用的木頭。

她們在食物貯藏處和帳篷附近把木頭堆得老高。當周遭的木頭撿光了，她們便回頭走進遠處的森林，背回更多捆木頭，直到天空落下雪花。有天早上，她們醒來時，四周已是一片鋪天蓋地的雪白。隨著冬天的腳步愈來愈近，她們待在帳篷裡以及坐在溫暖火堆旁的時間也愈來愈長。因為有充分的準備，日子似乎顯得輕鬆許多。

每天的生活很快地變得愈來愈規律：搜集木頭、檢查捕兔陷阱以及將雪融成清水。傍晚時分，兩個老婆婆就會坐在營火旁互相作伴。幾個月之前，她們忙得沒有時間回想發生在自己身上的事，即使腦袋裡偶爾想起，也置之不理。

但是現在每到傍晚，她們無事可做，不愉快的記憶就又不斷浮現腦海。很快地，兩人的話愈來愈少，都心事重重，凝視著那堆小小的營火。她們知道盡量不要去想那些拋棄她們的人比較好，但是被背叛的想法依然在腦中徘徊不去。

漆黑的夜晚變得愈來愈長，大地一片寂靜。她們得在白天多找點事來做，就用兔子皮毛做了很多衣物，像是手套、帽子、面罩。只是，即使兩個老婆婆讓自己忙於工作，仍然可以感覺到一股巨大的寂寞感，慢慢地將她們團團包圍。

第六章

部落人的哀傷

酋長站著環顧四周，眼睛因為深沉的哀傷而略顯蒼老。他的族人正處於絕望之中，眼睛和臉頰深陷在瘦可見骨的臉上，衣服破爛不堪，幾乎無法抵禦這刺骨的寒冷。許多人都被凍傷，幸運離他們遠去。即使如此絕望，他們仍然四處尋找獵物，不知不覺，回到了前一個冬天，他們拋棄兩個老婆婆的地方。

酋長回想起當時自己如何克制那股回頭去救老婆婆的衝動，心裡仍然很難過；但是若真的把她們帶回部落，可能會變成他最不該做的事。部落裡許多野心勃勃的年輕人會將此視為懦弱的行為，而且無可避免的是，部落的人也會因此認定他們的領導者不可倚

靠。不可以，這事絕對不能發生。酋長很清楚，領導權突然變動，會為部落帶

來比飢餓更大的傷害。當部落正在挨餓，不當的領導只會引發更大的災難。對

於自己當時差一點因為意志薄弱、感情用事而害了大家，酋長仍記憶猶新。

現在又是相同的情況，部落的人都在受苦，眼看又是毫無希望的冬天。拋

棄兩個老婆婆之後，他們走了很長一段艱困的路程，才碰到一小群野牛，這些

肉讓大家得以支撐到春天。然後他們開始獵捕魚、鴨子、麝鼠和水獺。但是就

在他們恢復打獵和曬乾食物的力氣時，夏天已然結束，該是部落考慮要遷移到

哪裡，好去尋找冬天肉類存糧的時光中度過。現在，他們再次碰到幾乎沒有食物

刻，整個秋天就在部落遷徙的時光中度過。酋長從來沒有經歷過運氣這麼差的時

可吃的情況。酋長心裡不斷交織著緊張和懷疑自己的情緒，不知道何時會因為

飢餓和疲勞而無法果斷做出決定，不知道自己還能支撐多久？他疲憊地看著

部落裡的人，大家似乎已經放棄生存的希望。他們不再用心聽他說話，只是眼

神空洞地看著他，好像他說的話沒有什麼意義。

決定回到拋棄兩個老婆婆的地方，是另一件讓酋長感到煩惱的事。當他帶

著大家回到這裡，沒有人抗議，但是酋長知道大家心裡都很驚訝。現在他們站著環顧四周，好像在等他說些什麼，又好像希望再看到那兩個老婆婆。酋長避開眾人的目光，不希望他們看出自己也同樣迷惑。這裡完全看不出曾經有人留下的痕跡，也沒有看到任何骨頭可以證明兩個老婆婆已經死亡。即使是動物把她們吃了也會吐出骨頭，只要有人死在這裡，一定會留下什麼。但是什麼都沒有，連可以替她們擋風遮雨的帳篷也不見蹤影。

在部落當中，有一個擔任嚮導的老人名叫達古，雖然比兩個老婆婆年輕，但仍被視為長者。他年輕的時候，一直擔任追蹤的工作，只是近來視力和追蹤技巧都大不如前。他仔細觀察一些別人不會發覺的地方。「也許她們離開了。」他壓低聲音說話，只打算讓酋長聽見。但因為四周一片寂靜，很多人都聽到了他的話，有些人也逐漸燃起希望，希望這兩個曾經受大家喜愛的老婆婆還活著。

營地設置妥當之後，酋長召來嚮導和三個部落裡最強壯的年輕獵人。「我不知道到底發生了什麼事，但是我有種感覺，事情並不是表面上看起來的那樣。我要你們到附近的營地，看看能找到什麼。」

酋長沒有說出心裡懷疑的事，但是他知道，嚮導和其他三個獵人應該會了解他的想法，特別是達古。在四季更迭的歲月中，他總是看護著酋長，對於酋長心裡想的事了然於胸。達古很尊敬酋長，他明白酋長因為自己在拋棄兩個老婆婆事件中所扮演的角色，一直自責不已，也看到了酋長臉上深深烙印著許多苦澀的皺紋，知道酋長討厭自己的軟弱。年老的達古嘆了一口氣，很清楚這種自我厭惡總有一天會爆發出來，但他不希望看到像酋長這樣一個好人因此毀了自己。是的，他會試著查明兩個老婆婆到底發生什麼事，即使徒勞無功。

四個男人離開很久之後，酋長仍凝視著他們遠去的方向。他找不到一個明確的原因來解釋，為什麼要把這麼多珍貴的精力和時間，浪費在也許是無謂的努力上。不過他心裡也的確有股奇怪的希望。希望什麼？他沒有答案。唯一能夠肯定的是，在這麼艱苦的時期，部落的人應該團結起來。上個冬天他們並沒有同心協力，沒有公平地對待自己和兩個老婆婆，而且從那天開始，部落裡的人就默默承受著痛苦。如果兩個老婆婆還活著就好了，但是酋長很清楚，這

星星婆婆的雪鞋 ★

樣的希望有多麼渺茫。那麼脆弱的兩個人，要如何在沒有食物、又沒有力氣打獵的情況下，度過這樣冷冽的寒冬呢？酋長雖然清楚這一點，但是仍不願輕易放棄這艱苦的幾個月來，一直抱持的小小希望。倘若找到兩個活著的老婆婆，將會給部落的人第二次選擇的機會，而那也許就是他最希望看到的事。

這四個男人都有長距離跑步的能耐。去年兩個老婆婆花了好幾天才到達的第一個營地，他們四個人只花一天就到了。除了無窮無盡的白雪和樹林，他們什麼也沒找到。艱困難行的小徑耗掉了有限的精力，因此他們決定在第一個營地過夜。當清晨的第一道曙光射出時，他們馬上起身，繼續向前奔跑。

當他們到達第二個營地時，白晝將盡，年輕的獵人沒有看到任何有人長久停留的證據，而開始覺得不耐煩。他們從小就被教導要尊重長輩，但是有時候卻認為自己懂得比長輩還多。雖然沒有大聲說出來，但是他們覺得這是在浪費寶貴的時間，應該將這個時間拿去獵捕麋鹿。

「我們現在回頭吧。」其中一個年輕人這樣提議，其他人很快地附和。

達古饒有興味地看著他們。真是沒有耐心啊！但是達古並沒有出聲批評，因為自己其實也和那些年輕人一樣開始覺得急躁。不過他沒有表現出來，反而說：「仔細看看你們的四周。」年輕的獵人不耐煩地看著他。

「仔細看看那些白樺樹。」達古非常堅持。那些人茫然地盯著樹木，看不出有什麼不對。達古嘆了一口氣。其中一個年輕人順著達古的目光望過去，注意到有些異樣。終於，他的眼睛因為驚訝而張大。「看那邊！」他說，手指著一棵白樺樹，上頭因為樹皮沒了而出現一片空白痕跡。接著他們發現像這樣的樹，廣泛散布在附近。樹皮被人很小心地剝掉，幾乎像是刻意這樣做，以求不被人發現。

「也許是另外一個部落。」其中一個人說。

「那他們為什麼要試圖隱藏樹上那些空白痕跡？」達古問。那個年輕人聳聳肩，無法回答。

接著達古下達指示。「在回去之前，」他說，「我們要搜索這個區域。」年輕人還來不及出聲抗議，達古已經用手指向不同的方向。「如果你們看到什麼不尋常的地方，回到這裡，我們再一起過去看看那是什麼。」雖然大家都累了，還是馬上開始搜尋，即使全都繃著臉，不相信兩個老婆婆還活著。

同時，達古朝著自己認為兩個老婆婆可能會去的方向走。「如果我很害怕被拋棄我的部落族人找到，我會走這個方向，」他自言自語，「走這個方向一點道理都沒有，因為離水畔愈來愈遠。但是在冬天，她們並不一定要仰賴水來生活，所以我想她們應該是走這個方向。」

達古走了很長一段距離，進入柳樹林以及高大的雲杉樹下。他在雪上艱難地行走，隨著距離愈來愈遠，愈覺得疲憊，心裡不禁懷疑自己的猜測。部落的人們都幾乎無法度過冬天了，兩個老婆婆又怎麼可能活下來？特別是這兩個老婆婆除了抱怨，什麼都不會。即使是小孩子叫著肚子餓，她們也能抱怨和批評。很多次達古都希望有人能讓她們閉嘴，但是從來沒有，直到一切失去控制的那個日子來臨。達古開始覺得自己只是在做沒有意義的搜尋，兩個老婆婆一定迷了路，死在路邊了，也或許在試著渡河的時候淹死了。

達古把所有的事情都想過一次，開始懷疑、產生負面想法。此時，他突然聞到一股氣味，在冬天清新如水的空氣中，一股淡淡的煙味竄入鼻子裡，又隨即消散不見。達古靜靜地站著，想再一次捕捉這股氣味，卻什麼也沒聞到。有一陣子他覺得會不會是自己的想像，也許只是附近的一個夏季火堆殘留在空氣中的味道。只是他不願意這麼想，慢慢的往後追蹤，直到再一次聞到那個味道。

氣味很淡，但是這一次達古知道，這不是夏季營火留下來的，不，這個煙味是新近的。他很興奮，先試著朝某個方向走去，然後再換一個方向，看看煙味是不是變得更加強烈。他確信味道是從附近的營火傳來的。他的臉因為綻開一個大大的笑容而皺在一起，因為他確定，兩個老婆婆還活著。

達古很快回到集合地點，找到那些先前等得不耐煩的年輕人。達古示意大家跟著他走。雖然不情願，但他們還是跟著達古一直走到入夜，時間似乎過了很久，終於達古抬起手，示意大家停下來。他抬高鼻子，要他們聞看看空氣裡的味道。這群年輕的獵人照著做了，卻什麼都沒有聞到。「你要我們聞什麼呢?」其中一個人問。

「繼續聞。」達古回答。他們再度嗅著，直到有一個人大喊，「我聞到煙味!」其他人也跟著興致高昂的四處走動，嗅著空氣。他們也聞到了，雖然他們仍心存懷疑，當中有一個年輕人問達古希望找到什麼。「我們等著看。」他只簡單說了這句話，一面帶著大家朝向煙味來源前進。

達古的眼睛緊張地看著黑漆漆的樹林，希望能找到一絲營火透出來的微弱光線。但是除了雲杉和柳樹的輪廓之外，他什麼也看不到。在天空點點繁星的微弱光線下，積雪沒有被人踏過的痕跡，一切都是那麼寧靜安詳。但是煙味可以證明，某人正紮營在某個地方。這個年老的追蹤者心中的篤定，就像血液就該奔流在血管中一般。他很確定那兩個老婆婆還活著，而且距離他們目前所在處很近。他掩不住心中的興奮，轉身對那群年輕人說：「兩個老婆婆就在附近。」

年輕人的背脊竄過一陣寒意，他們仍然不相信那兩個老婆婆還活著。

達古雙手圍成杯狀，向著寧靜的夜晚大聲呼喊兩個老婆婆的名字，並且表明自己的身分。接著他靜靜等待，卻只聽到自己喊出去的聲音被寂靜吞噬。

第七章

打破僵局

契日婭和莎已經準備休息。和往常一樣，做完日常雜務，吃過晚餐後，她們會在火堆旁坐下來聊天。這些日子她們常常聊到部落裡的人。寂寞和時間治癒了那段最痛苦的回憶，去年那個意外的背叛所造成的憎恨與恐懼，似乎在許多她們坐下來傾聽自己想法的夜晚中變得麻木。一切都像是個遙遠的夢。現在，她們肚子飽飽的，發現自己在舒適溫暖的帳篷中，談著她們有多麼想念部落的人。等到不知道該聊什麼，她們就靜靜坐著，各自想著心事。

四周的寧靜突然被劃破，兩個老婆婆聽到有人叫喊她們的名字。她們的目光從火堆的兩頭交會，知道剛剛聽到的聲音並不是憑空想像出來的。那個男人的聲音愈來愈大聲，並且說出自己的名字。她們認識這個老嚮導，認為也許可以相信他。但是其他人呢？契日婭先開口：「即使不回答，他們也可以找到我們。」

莎同意她的看法。「沒錯，他們會找到我們。」說話的同時，腦袋裡同時轉著許多想法。

「我們該怎麼辦？」契日婭緊張地快要掉下淚來。

莎想了一會兒，然後她說：「得讓他們知道我們在這裡。」看到契日婭的眼神逐漸變得歇斯底里，莎趕緊用平緩自信的聲音說：「我們必須勇敢面對他們，但是我的朋友，我們要做好可能會發生任何事的心理準備。」她停頓了一下，接著說：「甚至是死亡。」這麼說並沒有讓契日婭覺得舒服一點；莎從來沒看過她這麼害怕。

兩個老婆婆坐了很久，試著將所剩不多的勇氣通通聚集起來。她們知道自己沒辦法逃走。最後，莎慢慢起身，走入外頭寒冷的空氣中，嘶啞地大喊：「我們在這裡！」

達古一直很有耐心，很警覺地站著，那些年輕的獵人則懷疑地看著他。如果那是別人呢？也許是敵人？就在其中一個年輕人準備提出質疑時，他們在黑暗中聽到莎的回應。老嚮導的臉上綻放出滿滿笑容。果然沒錯！她們還活著。他們立刻朝著莎聲音傳來的方向走去。寒冷的空氣讓莎的聲音聽起來似乎很近，但是他們花了點時間，才走到她們的營地。

終於，他們愈來愈靠近帳篷外的營地火光。火堆旁站著兩個老婆婆，手上拿著長而銳利、看起來很危險的矛。達古不得不露出激賞的笑容，因為她們站著的姿態，就像兩個準備捍衛自己的戰士。「我們不是來傷害妳們的。」他向她們保證。

她們不太友善地瞪著他好一陣子，然後莎才說：「我相信你們沒有敵意。」

「但是你們為什麼來這裡？」達古呆站了一會兒，不確定該怎麼解釋。「酋長要我來這裡尋找你們。他相信妳們還活著。」

「為什麼？」契日婭疑惑地問。

「我不知道。」達古的回答很簡潔。的確，他很驚訝地發現，他根本就不

知道自己或是酋長曾經想過，一旦找到兩個老婆婆，該怎麼辦，因為很明顯，她們不會再信任他或是其他人。「我必須回去向酋長報告，我們已經找到妳們。」他說。兩個老婆婆很清楚這點。

「接下來呢？」莎問。

達古聳聳肩。「我不知道。但是不管發生什麼事，酋長都會保護妳們。」

「就像上次那樣保護嗎？」契日婭毫不客氣地問。

達古知道，如果他想的話，他和另外三個獵人，輕而易舉的就可以把這兩個人抓起來，奪下她們的武器。但是他覺得自己對她們愈來愈欣賞，因為兩個老婆婆已經做好準備去對抗任何必須面對的事。她們不再是以前他所認識的那兩個老婆婆。

「我向妳們保證。」他靜靜地說，而他們就這樣動也不動地站了很久，兩個老婆婆可以感覺到這句話的重大意義。

莎注意到這二人有多麼疲憊。即使達古以驕傲的姿態站著，仍然掩不住疲勞模樣。「你們看起來累壞了，」她的聲音透露著不情願，「進來裡面。」她帶著他們進入寬敞又溫暖的帳篷裡。

四個男人戒慎恐懼地走進帳篷，心知自己並不是受歡迎的客人。她們揮揮手要男人坐下，等到大家圍著火堆坐好，莎走到靠著帳篷邊的床後面挖了一會，拉出一個裝著魚的袋子，並且分給每個人一份魚乾。那些男人一面吃著魚，一面看著帳篷裡的一切，他們看到兩個老婆婆的床，是用新的兔毛編織而成。這兩個老婆婆看起來過得比部落的人還好。怎麼可能呢？等到他們把魚吃完，莎又端給每個人一碗熱騰騰的兔肉湯，大家都很高興地把湯喝了。

同時，契日婭坐在旁邊，惡狠狠地瞪著他們，讓他們全身都不舒服。他們很驚訝地發現，這兩個老婆婆不只活了下來，而且還健康強壯地坐在他們面前；而他們這些部落裡最強壯的人，卻總是沒吃飽。

他們在吃東西的時候，莎也注視著他們。她注意到他們試著慢慢把東西吞下，現在四周光線充足，從他們削瘦的臉龐，她可以看出這些人一直都吃得不好。契日婭也注意到這點，只是她的內心對這種多餘的打擾感到憤恨，所以一點都不可憐他們。吃完食物，達古滿懷期待看著她們，好像在等她們說話。

過了一會兒，還是沒有人肯打破沉默。最後達古說：「酋長相信妳們還活著，所以派我們來尋找。」契日婭生氣地哼了一聲。那些男人轉過頭去看她，她回以一個凶惡的表情後，別過頭去，無法相信這些人竟敢跑來找她們。莎當然也看得出來，他們來準沒好事。莎伸出手拍拍契日婭的手臂安撫她，接著轉向那些男人，淡淡地說：「是的，我們活下來了。」

契日婭的憤怒讓達古語塞。但是莎的怨恨似乎沒有那麼強烈，所以他避開契日婭如炬的目光，轉向莎說話。「我們正處於飢餓中，寒冷讓情況變得更糟。我們再一次碰到食物不足的問題，情況和留下妳們的那個時候一樣。但是如果酋長知道妳們都安好，他會希望妳們回到部落。酋長和部落裡大部分的人都與我有一樣的想法，我們很後悔那時對妳們所做的事。」

兩個老婆婆靜靜坐了很久，最後莎開口了：「可是你們也許會在我們最需要族人的時候，再一次拋棄我們？」達古花了一些時間想要怎麼回答，心想，要是酋長在這裡就好了，酋長對於回答這樣的問題比他有把握。

「我不敢說這樣的事情不會再發生。在艱困的時候，有的人會變得比惡狼更兇狠，而有的人會變得害怕懦弱，就像妳們被拋棄時的我一樣。」達古的聲音突然激動起來，但是他試著讓聲音平穩下來，繼續說，「我現在可以告訴妳們一件事。如果再發生那種事情，我會用我的生命保護妳們，只要我還活著。」

說話的同時，達古在這兩個他曾經認為沒用又虛弱的老婆婆身上體會到，他已經重新發現了自己內在的力量。這股力量曾在去年冬天時離開了他，現在不知為何，他再也不相信自己會變得年老衰弱。絕對不會！

年輕人一直安靜坐著，仔細聆聽這幾位長者之間的談話。此時，其中一個人用年輕熱情的聲音說：「我，也會保護妳們，如果有任何人想再一次傷害妳們。」每個人都驚訝地看著他。接著他的同伴也發誓要保護兩個老婆婆，因為他們親眼目睹這兩個人奇蹟似地活了下來，同時也對長者更多份尊敬的心。兩個老婆婆可以感覺到，自己的內心因為族人的話語而軟化，但是不信任的感覺仍然存在。即使她們相信眼前這些人，對於其他人，她們還是不能肯定。

兩個老婆婆聚在一起悄悄討論著。「我們可以相信他們嗎？」契日婭問。

莎考慮了一會兒，然後點點頭，溫柔地說：「可以。」

「其他的人怎麼辦？假如他們知道了我們貯藏的食物？妳覺得他們看到這麼多食物時會不會退縮？看看這些人有多飢餓。去年他們不尊重我們，現在妳卻願意讓他們來！我的朋友，我擔心他們會把食物拿走，而不管我們願不願意。」契日婭說。莎已經想過這點，但是她並不害怕，反而回答：「我們必須記得他們正在受苦。沒錯，他們那時的確太快拋棄我們，但是現在已經證明他們是錯的。我們必須將志得意滿放在一旁，並且記得他們正在受苦。就算不為大人，也要為小孩子想想。妳能忘了妳的孫子嗎？」

契日婭知道她的朋友跟平時一樣說得很有道理。不行，她不能這麼自私，不能讓她的孫子挨餓，而自己卻有這麼多的食物。當兩個老婆婆悄悄細聲交談時，達古他們很有耐心地等待著。

莎不只是口頭上說說，因為她很清楚，契日婭仍然對於即將發生的事情感到害怕，而且需要信心去面對未來。「他們並不知道我們為自己準備得有多好，」她說，「但是等到明天天亮時，他們就會看到，然後我們就會知道他們說的話是不是真的。但是記得這件事，我的朋友。如果他們再一次拋棄我們，我們還是能活下去。而如果他們說的是真心話，那麼也許在未來更艱難的狀況來臨時，我們可以成為鼓勵他們的力量。」

契日婭點頭同意。有那麼一會兒時間，當她看著這些部落裡來的人，感覺到以前那股恐懼再度浮現，而忘了新生的力量。契日婭非常讚許地看著她的朋友，莎似乎總是知道該說什麼。

那天晚上在帳篷裡，她們和老嚮導交換著彼此的故事，年輕人則是尊敬地靜靜聆聽著。達古將部落拋棄兩個老婆婆之後的事，一五一十道來。他提到那些死去的人，大多數是小孩子。她們聽著達古說的故事，淚水盈眶，因為她們一直很疼愛某些人，而那些人不幸就在其中。她們不忍去想像那些這麼年輕、可憐的孩子在死前要受多少苦。

達古說完故事後，莎把她們如何活下來的經過告訴他。旁邊的年輕人聽得五味雜陳。她所說的故事聽起來無法置信，但是她們好端端站在這裡的事實，卻是最好的證據。莎並不在意那些男人臉上的敬畏之色。她將故事娓娓道來，回顧著她和契日婭共同度過的這個多事之秋。她把貯藏了許多食物的事，當作故事的結尾告訴他們，這些來訪的人眼睛頓時亮了起來。

「當我們第一次聽到你的聲音，就知道可以相信你。我們也很清楚，如果你能夠在晚上找到我們，那麼你只要花一點點的時間，就可以找到我們的食物貯藏處。這就是為什麼我要現在告訴你。我知道你對我們沒有惡意。」莎直截了當地向達古說。「但是部落裡的人呢？如果他們會做出拋棄我們這樣的事情，那麼對於拿走我們的東西，也不會有什麼感覺。他們會認為我們又虛弱又年老，根本不需要這麼多存糧。我現在並不怪他們曾經做過的事，因為我們知道飢餓會讓一個人變成什麼樣子。但是這些食物是我們辛勤工作才換來的，即使知道這些食物用來過冬的確太多，但無論如何還是先儲存下來再說，也許是因為我們覺得會發生像今天這樣的情形吧！」莎停頓了一下，思考有沒有什麼話還沒有講。然後她繼續說：「我們會跟部落的人一起分享這些食物，但是他們不可以貪心，想要拿走所有的食物，因為我們會為這些食物奮戰到死。」

這些男人靜靜坐著，聽莎用強烈激昂的聲音說話。然後她開出條件：「你們要待在舊的營地，我們不希望看到任何人，除了你之外，」莎指著達古說，「還有酋長。我們會給你們食物，而且我希望部落能夠以更艱難的日子就要來臨的心態，節省地吃這些食物。這是我們能夠為你們做的事。」達古點頭同意，並用平靜的聲音說：「我會將這個訊息帶回去給酋長。」

等到大家把該說的話都說了，兩個老婆婆請那兩人睡在帳篷的另一邊。這麼長的時間以來，她們第一次覺得放鬆。在過去漫長的數月間，她們害怕很多事情。現在她們腦中的那些狼群和其他獵食者的畫面漸漸消失，兩個老婆婆無憂無慮地沉沉睡去。

她們不再孤獨。

第八章

新的開始

　　就在那群男人隔天離開前，她們將大捆的魚乾包好，數量足以讓部落的人恢復旅行的力量。同一時刻，酋長緊張地等待著，很擔心派出去的人不知是否出了什麼事，但是心裡仍抱持著希望，不讓那種想法占據自己的腦袋。當那些男人回來時，酋長很快召開會議，讓他們述說這段時間發生的事。

　　老嚮導將他們發現的事情告訴眼前震驚的人們。當故事說完，他告訴族人，兩個老婆婆並不相信、也不願意看到他們。達古告訴大家她們所開出的條件。幾分鐘的沉默之後，酋長說：「我們會尊重她們的意願，不同意的人必須要打贏我才行。」

　　達古很快加入酋長這一邊：「幾個年輕

人和我都會站在你這邊。」那些曾經建議將兩個老婆婆拋棄的會議成員，此時覺得非常羞愧。最後，其中一個人說：「我們拋棄她們是錯的，她們已經證明了這一點。現在我們將以尊敬之心回報她們。」

酋長對所有人宣布這件事情，部落同意遵照兩個老婆婆的要求。部落的人吃了魚乾，恢復體力之後，便開始打包行李，因為他們等不及想看看兩個老婆婆。在這個艱難的時期，她們活下來的消息讓整個部落充滿希望和敬畏。契日婭的女兒歐姿希‧內麗忍不住哭了出來，她以為她的母親已經死了，雖然聽到消息後大大鬆了一口氣，卻也明白她的母親永遠不會原諒她。旭盧勃‧祖非常高興。這個年輕的男孩立刻把東西收拾好，準備上路。

整個部落花了一些時間，才到達那個白樺樹皮被剝掉的營地。酋長和達古已經先行和兩個老婆婆碰面。當他們來到兩個老婆婆的營地時，酋長必須壓抑自己上前擁抱她們的衝動。她們用不信任的眼神看著他。他們先坐下來說話，兩個老婆婆告訴酋長對於部落的期待，酋長則回答大家會尊重她們的希望。

「我們會給部落夠吃的食物。等到食物快吃完的時候，我們會再多給你一點，一次給你一小部分。」莎這樣告訴酋長，酋長謙遜地點著頭。

他們會面後隔天，部落才到達新的營地。他們將行李拆開，架起帳篷，酋長則和他的手下帶著一捆捆魚乾和兔皮衣物回來。達古看到她們搜集了大量兔皮衣物，所以大膽將部落裡衣服不足的情形告知兩個老婆婆。兩個老婆婆都很清楚，她們絕對用不了這麼多在閒暇時所做的手套、面罩、毯子和背心，所以願意把這些東西和需要的人分享。部落的人在新營地安定下來，肚子也不再因為飢餓而咕嚕作響，他們對於兩個老婆婆感到愈來愈好奇。但是族人被禁止靠近老婆婆的營地。

寒冷的天氣來臨後，部落的人很小心地分配老婆婆給的食物。接著獵人們捕殺到一隻大麋鹿，並且拖了很遠的距離回到營地，所有的人都為接下來的美好時光歡呼慶祝。

這段時間，酋長和達古每天輪流去探望兩個老婆婆。後來兩個老婆婆也很好奇部落的狀況。酋長希望她們答應，讓部落的人來探訪。契日婭很快說不，因為她還無法放下她的驕傲。但是後來兩個老婆婆談到這件事時，她們都承認已經做好有人來訪的心理準備。對契日婭來說特別是這樣，因為她非常想念家人。隔天酋長來看老婆婆的時候，她們將決定告訴他。很快就有人來拜訪老婆婆。一開始她們很膽小，沒有什麼自信。但是幾次之後，她們愈來愈能輕鬆聊天，沒多久帳篷裡就傳出笑聲和快樂的交談聲。每一次有人來拜訪，都會帶著麋鹿肉和動物皮毛當禮物，而兩個老婆婆也都欣然收下。

部落的人和老婆婆之間的關係變得愈來愈融洽。雙方都經歷一番痛苦掙扎才學到一件事：人都有自己不知道的一面。部落的人一直以為自己很強壯，但他們也有脆弱的一面；而兩個老婆婆原先被認為是最無助、最沒用的人，但她們卻證明了自己的堅強。現在，雙方之間有了不需言傳的了解。部落的人也發現，自己會來尋求兩個老婆婆的忠告，並學習新的事物。他們現在明白，因為兩個老婆婆活了這麼久的時間，她們知道的事情，確實比部落其他人想像得多。

老婆婆的營地每天都有訪客來來去去。他們離開之後許久，契日婭會站著凝視他們遠去的身影。莎看著她，心裡很同情她的朋友，因為她知道契日婭希

望能見到女兒和孫子，但是他們沒有來。契日婭的心裡一直藏著一股恐懼，擔心是不是有什麼厄運發生在他們身上，而部落的人沒有告訴她，而她又害怕得不敢開口問。

有一天，契日婭在搜集木頭時，身後響起一個溫柔的聲音：「我來拿我的小斧頭。」契日婭慢慢站起來，手上的木頭在轉過身時全都掉到地上，但她卻渾然不覺。他們互相凝視，彷彿正在夢中，不敢相信眼前所見。他們滿心歡喜地看著對方，此時無聲勝有聲。契日婭毫不猶豫地向前擁抱她心愛的年輕男孩。

莎站在一旁，笑看著這快樂重逢的一幕。旭盧勃・祖抬頭看著莎，走向她，給了莎一個溫柔的擁抱。莎的內心充滿疼愛之情，也為這個年輕人感到驕傲。

不過，契日婭還在想她的女兒。莎的內心充滿疼愛之情，這一切莎都看在眼裡，很清楚為什麼她的朋友即使食物充足，看起來還是很悲傷。有一天，另外一個孫子來訪後，莎走過去緊握契日婭的手。「她會來的。」莎簡短地說。契日婭雖然不是非常相信，但仍然點了點頭。

冬天已近尾聲。現在兩個營地之間已經踩出一條平整的道路。部落的人都等不及要來和兩個老婆婆作伴，特別是小孩子，他們會在營地裡歡笑嬉鬧，而兩個老婆婆則坐在帳篷旁看著。她們很高興能夠活下來看到這幕歡樂的景象。

旭盧勃・祖每天都會過來，像以前一樣幫祖母做一些日常雜務，並且聽她們說故事。有一天契日婭終於等不下去，鼓起勇氣問：「我的女兒在哪裡？為對她們來說，生活不再和以前一樣枯燥乏味。

什麼她沒有來？」年輕男孩很誠實地回答：「她很羞愧，祖母。她覺得自從背棄妳的那天開始，妳就一直憎恨著她。從我們分開後，她每天都以淚洗面。」

男孩一面說，一面張開手抱住契日婭。「我很擔心，因為悲傷讓她日漸衰老。」

契日婭坐著聽孫子說話，心卻飛到了女兒身上。「沒錯，她之前真的非常生氣。她不知道自己這個母親是怎麼當的？這麼多年來，她訓練女兒要堅強，但最後卻發現一切都是徒勞。不過契日婭想到，她的女兒不該擔起這一切的罪責，畢竟部落裡每個人都參與了這件事，而女兒的行動是出自恐懼，她擔心兒子和母親的生命，事情就是這麼簡單。契日婭也知道女兒勇敢的留下了一捆皮條，把這麼有價值的東西留給兩個被認為必死無疑的老婆婆，一定會被視為是一種不智的浪費。

是的，她可以原諒女兒。契日婭甚至該跟她說聲謝謝，如果不是女兒送了那捆皮條，她們也許沒辦法活到現在。契日婭回過神來，才發現她的孫子等著她說些什麼。她伸手抱住他的肩頭，輕輕的拍著說：「我的孫子，請告訴我的女兒，我並不恨她。」男孩的臉緩和下來，因為他已經好幾個月都在擔心母親和祖母。現在，所有事情幾乎都回到從前。他毫不猶豫給祖母一個熱烈的擁抱，然後衝出帳篷，馬不停蹄地跑回家。

回到營地時，他已經上氣不接下氣。他衝向他的媽媽。這個興奮的年輕人一面喘息一面說：「媽媽！祖母想要見妳！她告訴我，她已經不再恨了！」歐姿希·內麗非常驚訝。她沒有想到會這樣，有一陣子，她的雙腿發軟，不得不坐下來。她的身體顫抖，再一次看著兒子，「這是真的嗎？」她問。「是的。」

旭盧勃·祖回答，而他的母親看得出他說的是實話。

一開始，她提不起勇氣去找契日婭，因為她還是有罪惡感。但是在兒子溫柔的堅持下，歐姿希·內麗鼓起勇氣，走了長長的一段路到達母親的營地，而她的兒子陪伴在旁。當他們到達營地時，兩個老婆婆正在帳篷外聊天。莎先看到來訪的人，然後契日婭才轉身去看是什麼讓莎安靜下來。當她看到女兒，嘴巴微張卻吐不出一個字。她們沒有說話，靜靜注視著對方，一直到契日婭走向歐姿希·內麗，並緊緊抱著她哭泣。她們身旁所有的人事物似乎在此刻都消失無蹤。

莎站在一旁，雙手環抱著旭盧勃·祖，淚眼盈眶地看著這一對母女找到了她們以為已經永遠失去的親情。然後契日婭轉身走進帳篷，回來的時候將手上一小捆東西塞到她女兒手裡。歐姿希·內麗看到那是皮條，她不太懂母親為什麼這麼做。直到契日婭靠過來，在她的耳邊輕聲說了一些話。歐姿希·內麗臉上露出驚訝的表情，過了一會她也面帶微笑。再一次，兩人緊緊擁抱著彼此。

重新聚首後，酋長指定兩個老婆婆擔任部落裡的榮譽職位。一開始，部落的人希望能夠盡可能幫助兩個老婆婆，但是她們不肯接受太多協助，因為她們很喜歡新發現的獨立感，所以部落的人聆聽她們說的話，以示尊重。

更艱難的時節就要來臨，在北方這片寒冷的土地上，這是很自然的事，但部落的人心存希望。他們從兩個老婆婆身上學到教訓，不再拋棄年老的族人，並持續續關心、敬愛著這兩個老婆婆，直到她們安詳快樂的離開人世。

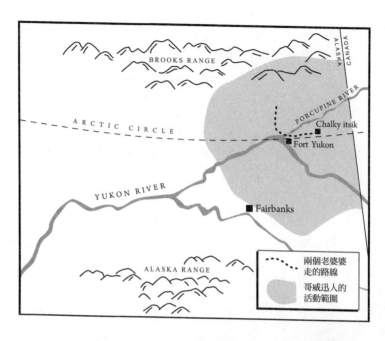

關於哥威迅人

威兒瑪・瓦歷斯在《星星婆婆的雪鞋》一書中所描寫的族群，是散居在目前育空堡（Fort Yukon）和查爾基齊克（Chalkyitsik）區域的哥威迅人（Gwich'in）部落的一支。哥威迅人是阿拉斯加的阿撒巴斯卡（Athabaskan）十一個不同部落中的一個，居住於阿拉斯加州西邊內陸的育空河、波丘派恩河（Porcupine）與塔納那河（Tanana）沿岸。

每一個部落都有自己的方言，但許多阿撒巴斯卡人不僅能通曉其他部落的語言，更和納瓦約（Navajo）與阿帕契（Apache）印地安人部落的語言有著相同的語源。一般認為，所有的印地安人都是在冰河時期之初，跨越東西伯利亞進入阿拉斯加的亞洲人。

阿撒巴斯卡人散布在阿拉斯加內陸，大部分居住於布魯克斯山脈（Brooks Range）和阿拉斯加山脈（Alaska Range）之間。居住在主要河川系統的部落，仰賴一年一度的鮭魚迴游維生，而住在更遠的內陸部落，像是哥威迅人，則以成群的大型動物如麋鹿和野牛，和小型動物如兔子和松鼠作為主要食物來源。

歷史上，每一支阿拉斯加的阿撒巴斯卡部落都有一片從以前傳承下來的領地。每一個部落的獵人對於領地的範圍都相當熟稔，部分的原因是，一般認為在其他部落的領地上活動是具有危險性的。領土範圍是依這個部落打獵和捕魚的區域劃定。侵入其他部落領地的行為是很罕見的，但是一旦發生入侵行為，則通常免不了產生暴力爭鬥。

阿撒巴斯卡人的遷徙自然與他們跟隨食物來源的生活方式有關。他們無法只是坐在原地，等著食物自己送上門，因為一不小心，挨餓和飢荒便隨之而來。所以他們到處移動，並且根據季節變化，在一些預料可能豐收的漁獵地點建立營地。

阿撒巴斯卡人有時候會碰上飢荒，因為土地無法提供足夠的食物給部落。雖然那不算是每天都會出現的生存威脅，但是飢荒的可能性是眾所周知的現實。部落的人們刻苦地生活著，畢竟北極地區的森林並非易於謀生的地方。生活裡包含了許多任務和工作，一旦疏於執行，就可能導致大難臨頭。

至一九〇〇年左右，阿撒巴斯卡人開始遷入更多永久營地或村莊。這個結果的背後有許多原因，例如人口由於疾病肆虐而減少，毛皮貿易的影響，到達交易站點的難易度，以及後來必須就學的強制規定等。時至今日，即使許多人已經從事支薪的工作，以大地維生的生存方式仍然是大多數阿拉斯加的阿撒巴斯卡人生活中重要的一部分。

故事盒子 18

星星婆婆的雪鞋
馴鹿民族流傳兩千年的勇氣傳說【30 週年暢銷紀念版‧中英雙語】

作 者	威兒瑪‧瓦歷斯 Velma Wallis	
繪 者	詹姆斯‧格蘭特 James Grant	
譯 者	王聖棻、魏婉琪	

野人文化股份有限公司

社 長 張瑩瑩
總 編 輯 蔡麗真
副總編輯 陳瑾璇
責任編輯 林毓茹、李怡庭
行銷經理 林麗紅
行銷企劃 李映柔
封面設計 鄭宇斌
內頁排版 奧嘟嘟工作室、洪素貞

出 版 野人文化股份有限公司
發 行 遠足文化事業股份有限公司(讀書共和國出版集團)
　　　　 地址:231 新北市新店區民權路 108-2 號 9 樓
　　　　 電話:(02)2218-1417　傳真:(02)8667-1065
　　　　 電子信箱:service@bookrep.com.tw
　　　　 網址:www.bookrep.com.tw
　　　　 郵撥帳號:19504465 遠足文化事業股份有限公司
　　　　 客服專線:0800-221-029
法律顧問 華洋法律事務所蘇文生律師
印 製 呈靖彩藝股份有限公司
初 版 2007 年 09 月
二 版 2013 年 03 月
三 版 2024 年 10 月

國家圖書館出版品預行編目資料

星星婆婆的雪鞋 / 威兒瑪‧瓦歷斯 (Velma Wallis) 著;王
聖棻、魏婉琪譯 .-- 三版 .-- 新北市:野人文化股份有限
公司出版:遠足文化事業股份有限公司發行, 2024.10
　面; 公分 .--(故事盒子;18)
　譯自:Two Old Women
　ISBN 978-626-7555-01-9(平裝)
　ISBN 978-626-7555-99-3(EPUB)
　ISBN 978-626-7555-00-2(PDF)

874.57　　　　　　　　　　　　113011410

星星婆婆的雪鞋

野人文化　　野人文化
官方網頁　　讀者回函

線上讀者回函專用
QR CODE,你的寶
貴意見,將是我們
進步的最大動力。

Two Old Women

An Alaska Legend
of Betrayal, Courage
and Survival

Velma Wallis

CONTENTS

CHAPTER 1

Hunger and Cold Take their Toll

The air stretched tight, quiet and cold over the vast land. Tall spruce branches hung heavily laden with snow, awaiting distant spring winds. The frosted willows seemed to tremble in the freezing temperatures.

Far off in this seemingly dismal land were bands of people dressed in furs and animal skins, huddled close to small campfires. Their weather-burnt faces were stricken with looks of hopelessness as they faced starvation, and the future held little promise of better days.

These nomads were The People of the arctic region of Alaska, always on the move in search of food. Where the caribou and other migrating animals roamed, The People followed. But the deep cold of winter presented special problems. The moose, their favorite source of food, took refuge from the penetrating cold by staying in one place, and were difficult to find. Smaller, more accessible animals such as rabbits and tree squirrels could

not sustain a large band such as this one. And during the cold spells, even the smaller animals either disappeared in hiding or were thinned by predators, man and animal alike. So during this unusually bitter chill in the late fall, the land seemed void of life as the cold hovered menacingly.

During the cold, hunting required more energy than at other times. Thus, the hunters were fed first, as it was their skills on which The People depended. Yet, with so many to feed, what food they had was depleted quickly. Despite their best efforts, many of the women and children suffered from malnutrition, and some would die of starvation.

In this particular band were two old women cared for by The People for many years. The older woman's name was Ch'idzigyaak, for she reminded her parents of a chickadee bird when she was born. The other woman's name was Sa', meaning "star," because at the time of her birth her mother had been looking at the fall night sky, concentrating on the distant stars to take her mind away from the painful labor contractions.

The chief would instruct the younger men to set up shelters for these two old women each time the band arrived at a new campsite, and to provide them with wood and water. The younger women pulled the two elder women's possessions from one camp to the next and, in turn, the old women tanned animal skins for those who helped them. The arrangement worked well.

However, the two old women shared a character flaw un-

usual for people of those times. Constantly they complained of aches and pains, and they carried walking sticks to attest to their handicaps. Surprisingly, the others seemed not to mind, despite having been taught from the days of their childhood that weakness was not tolerated among the inhabitants of this harsh motherland. Yet, no one reprimanded the two women, and they continued to travel with the stronger ones — until one fateful day.

On that day, something more than the cold hung in the air as The People gathered around their few flickering fires and listened to the chief. He was a man who stood almost a head taller than the other men. From within the folds of his parka ruff he spoke about the cold, hard days they were to expect and of what each would have to contribute if they were to survive the winter.

Then, in a loud, clear voice he made a sudden announcement: "The council and I have arrived at a decision." The chief paused as if to find the strength to voice his next words. "We are going to have to leave the old ones behind."

His eyes quickly scanned the crowd for reactions. But the hunger and cold had taken their toll, and The People did not seem to be shocked. Many expected this to happen, and some thought it for the best. In those days, leaving the old behind in times of starvation was not an unknown act, although in this band it was happening for the first time. The starkness of the primitive land seemed to demand it, as the people, to survive, were forced to imitate some of the ways of the animals. Like the

younger, more able wolves who shun the old leader of the pack, these people would leave the old behind so that they could move faster without the extra burden.

The older woman, Ch'idzigyaak, had a daughter and a grandson among the group. The chief looked into the crowd for them and saw that they, too, had shown no reaction. Greatly relieved that the unpleasant announcement had been made without incident, the chief instructed everyone to pack immediately. Meanwhile, this brave man who was their leader could not bring himself to look at the two old women, for he did not feel so strong now.

The chief understood why The People who cared for the old women did not raise objections. In these hard times, many of the men became frustrated and were angered easily, and one wrong thing said or done could cause uproar and make matters worse. So it was that the weak and beaten members of the tribe kept what dismay they felt to themselves, for they knew that the cold could bring on a wave of panic followed by cruelty and brutality among people fighting for survival.

In the many years the women had been with the band, the chief had come to feel affection for them. Now, he wanted to be away as quickly as possible so that the two old women could not look at him and make him feel worse than he had ever felt in his life.

The two women sat old and small before the campfire with their chins held up proudly, disguising their shock. In their

younger days they had seen very old people left behind, but they never expected such a fate. They stared ahead numbly as if they had not heard the chief condemn them to a certain death — to be left alone to fend for themselves in a land that understood only strength. Two weak old women stood no chance against such a rule. The news left them without words or action and no way to defend themselves.

Of the two, Ch'idzigyaak was the only one with a family — a daughter, Ozhii Nelii, and a grandson, Shrub Zhuu. She waited for her daughter to protest, but none came, and a deeper sense of shock overcame her. Not even her own daughter would try to protect her. Next to her, Sa' also was stunned. Her mind reeled and, though she wanted to cry out, no words came. She felt as if she were in a terrible nightmare where she could neither move nor speak.

As the band slowly trudged away, Ch'idzigyaak's daughter went over to her mother, carrying a bundle of babiche — thickly stripped raw moosehide that served many purposes. She hung her head in shame and grief, for her mother refused to acknowledge her presence. Instead, Ch'idzigyaak stared unflinchingly ahead.

Ozhii Nelii was in deep turmoil. She feared that, if she defended her mother, The People would settle the matter by leaving her behind and her son, too. Worse yet, in their famished state, they might do something even more terrible. She could not chance it.

With those frightening thoughts, Ozhii Nelii silently begged with sorrowful eyes for forgiveness and understanding as she gently laid the babiche down in front of her rigid parent. Then she slowly turned and walked away with a heaviness in her heart, knowing she had just lost her mother.

The grandson, Shrub Zhuu, was deeply disturbed by the cruelty. He was an unusual boy. While the other boys competed for their manhood by hunting and wrestling, this one was content to help provide for his mother and the two old women. His behavior seemed to be outside of the structure of the band's organization handed down from generation to generation. In this case, the women did most of the burdensome tasks such as pulling the well-packed toboggans. In addition, much other time-consuming work was expected to be done by the women while the men concentrated on hunting so that the band could survive. No one complained, for that was the way things were and always had been.

Shrub Zhuu held much respect for the women. He saw how they were treated and he disapproved. And while it was explained to him over and over, he never understood why the men did not help the women. But his training told him that he never was to question the ways of The People, for that would be disrespectful. When he was younger, Shrub Zhuu was not afraid to voice his opinions on this subject, for youth and innocence were his guardians. Later, he learned that such behavior invited punishment. He felt the pain of the silent treatment when even

his mother refused to speak to him for days. So Shrub Zhuu learned that it caused less pain to think about certain things than to speak out about them.

Although he thought abandoning the helpless old women was the worst thing The People could do, Shrub Zhuu was struggling with himself. His mother saw the turmoil raging in his eyes and she knew that he was close to protesting. She went to him quickly and whispered urgently into his ear not to think of it, for the men were desperate enough to commit any kind of cruel action. Shrub Zhuu saw the men's dark faces and knew this to be true, so he held his tongue even as his heart continued to rage rebelliously.

In those days, each young boy was trained to care for his weapons, sometimes better than he cared for his loved ones, for the weapons were to be his livelihood when he became a man. When a boy was caught handling his weapon the wrong way or for the wrong purpose, it resulted in harsh punishment. As he grew older, the boy would learn the power of his weapon and how much significance it had, not only for his own survival but also for that of his people.

Shrub Zhuu threw all this training and thoughts of his own safety to the winds. He took from his belt a hatchet made of sharpened animal bones bound tightly together with hardened babiche and stealthily placed it high in the thick boughs of a bushy young spruce tree, well concealed from the eyes of The People.

As Shrub Zhuu's mother packed their things, he turned toward his grandmother. Though she seemed to look right through him, Shrub Zhuu made sure no one was watching as he pointed to his empty belt, then toward the spruce tree.

Once more he gave his grandmother a look of hopelessness, and reluctantly turned and walked away to join the others, wishing with a sinking feeling that he could do something miraculous to end this nightmarish day.

The large band of famished people slowly moved away, leaving the two women sitting in the same stunned position on their piled spruce boughs. Their small fire cast a soft orange glow onto their weathered faces. A long time passed before the cold brought Ch'idzigyaak out other stupor. She was aware other daughter's helpless gesture but believed that her only child should have defended her even in the face of danger. The old woman's heart softened as she thought other grandson. How could she bear hard feelings toward one so young and gentle? The others made her angry, especially her daughter! Had she not trained her to be strong? Hot, unbidden tears ran from her eyes.

At that moment, Sa' lifted her head in time to see her friend's tears. A rush of anger surged within her. How dare they? Her cheeks burned with the humiliation. She and the other old woman were not close to dying! Had they not sewed and tanned for what the people gave them? They did not have to be carried from camp to camp. They were neither helpless

nor hopeless. Yet they had been condemned to die.

Her friend had seen eighty summers, she, seventy-five. The old ones she had seen left behind when she was young were so close to death that some were blind and could not walk. Now here she was, still able to walk, to see, to talk, yet... bah! Younger people these days looked for easier ways out of hard times. As the cold air smothered the campfire, Sa' came alive with a greater fire within her, almost as if her spirit had absorbed the energy from the now-glowing embers of the campfire. She went to the tree and retrieved the hatchet, smiling softly as she thought of her friend's grandson. She sighed as she walked toward her companion, who had not stirred.

Sa' looked up at the blue sky. To an experienced eye, the blue this time of winter meant cold. Soon it would be colder yet as night approached. With a worried frown on her face, Sa' kneeled beside her friend and spoke in a gentle but firm voice. "My friend," she said and paused, hoping for more strength than she felt. "We can sit here and wait to die. We will not have long to wait...

"Our time of leaving this world should not come for a long time yet," she added quickly when her friend looked up with panic-stricken eyes. "But we will die if we just sit here and wait. This would prove them right about our helplessness."

Ch'idzigyaak listened with despair. Knowing that her friend was dangerously close to accepting a fate of death from cold and hunger, Sa' spoke more urgently. "Yes, in their own

way they have condemned us to die! They think that we are too old and useless. They forget that we, too, have earned the right to live! So I say if we are going to die, my friend, let us die trying, not sitting."

CHAPTER 2

Let us Die Trying

Ch'idzigyaak sat quietly as if trying to make up her confused mind. A small feeling of hope sparked in. the blackness of her being as she listened to her friend's strong words. She felt the cold stinging her cheeks where her tears had fallen, and she listened to the silence that The People left behind. She knew that what her friend said was true, that within this calm, cold land waited a certain death if they did nothing for themselves. Finally, more in desperation than in determination she echoed her friend's words, "Let us die trying." With that, her friend helped her up off the sodden branches.

The women gathered sticks to build the fire and they added pieces of fungus that grew large and dry on fallen cottonwood trees to keep it smoldering. They went around to other campfires to salvage what embers they could find. As they packed to travel, the migrating bands in these times preserved hot coals in hardened mooseskin sacks or birchbark containers filled with

ash in which the embers pulsated, ready to spark the next camp-fire.

As night approached, the women cut thin strips from the bundle of babiche, fashioning them into nooses the size of a rabbit's head. Then, despite their weariness, the women managed to make some rabbit snares, which they immediately set out.

The moon hung big and orange on the horizon as they trudged through the knee-deep snow, searching in the dimness for signs of rabbit life. It was hard to see, and what rabbits existed stayed quiet in the cold weather. But they found several old, hardened rabbit trails frozen solid beneath the trees and arching willows. Ch'idzigyaak tied a babiche noose to a long, thick willow branch and placed it across one of the trails. She made little fences of willows and spruce boughs on each side of the noose to guide the rabbit through the snare. The two women set a few more snares but felt little hope that even one rabbit would be caught.

On their way back to the camp, Sa' heard something skitter lightly along the bark of a tree. She stood very still, motioning her friend to do the same. Both women strained to hear the sound once more in the silence of the night. On a tree not far from them, silhouetted in the now-silvery moonlight, they saw an adventurous tree squirrel. Sa' slowly reached to her belt for the hatchet. With her eyes on the squirrel and her movements deliberately slow, she aimed the hatchet toward this target that

represented survival. The animal's small head came up instantly and as Sa' moved her hand to throw, the squirrel darted up the tree. Sa' foresaw this, and, aiming a little higher, ended the small animal's life in one calculating throw with skill and hunting knowledge that she had not used in many seasons.

Ch'idzigyaak let out a deep sigh of relief. The moon's light shone on the younger woman's smiling face as she said in a proud yet shaky voice, "Many times I have done that, but never did I think I would do it again."

Back at the camp, the women boiled the squirrel meat in snow water and drank the broth, saving the small portion of meat to be eaten later, for they knew that otherwise, this could be their last meal.

The two women had not eaten for some time because The People had tried to conserve what little food they had. Now they realized why precious food had not been given to them. Why waste food on two who were to die? Trying not to think about what had happened, the two women filled their empty stomachs -with the warm squirrel broth and settled down in their tents for the night.

The shelter was made of two large caribou hides wrapped around three long sticks shaped into a kind of triangle. Inside were thickly piled spruce boughs covered with many fur blankets. The women were aware that, although they had been left behind to fend for themselves, The People had done them a good deed by leaving them with all their possessions. They

suspected that the chief was responsible for this small kindness. Other less noble members of the band would have decided that the two women soon would die and would have pilfered everything except for the warm fur and skin clothing they wore. With these confusing thoughts lingering in their minds, the two frail women dozed.

The moonlight shone silently upon the frozen earth as life whispered throughout the land, broken now and then by a lone wolf's melancholy howl. The women's eyes twitched in tired, troubled dreams, and soft helpless moans escaped from their lips. Then a cry rang out somewhere in the night as the moon dipped low on the western horizon. Both women awoke at once, hoping that the awful screech was a part of her nightmare. Again the wail was heard. This time, the women recognized it as the sound of something caught in one of their snares. They were relieved. Fearing that other predators would beat them to their catch, the women hurriedly dressed and rushed to their snare sets. There they saw a small, trembling rabbit that lay partially strangled as it eyed them warily. Without hesitation, Sa' went to the rabbit, put one hand around its neck, felt for the beating heart, and squeezed until the small struggling animal went limp. After Sa' reset the snare, they went back to the camp, each feeling a thread of new hope.

Morning came, but brought no light to this far northern land. Ch'idzigyaak awoke first. She slowly kindled the fire into a flame as she care- fully added more wood. When the fire had

died out during the cold night, frost from their warm breathing had accumulated on the walls of caribou skins.

Sighing in dull exasperation, Ch'idzigyaak went outside where the northern lights still danced above, and the stars winked in great numbers. Ch'idzigyaak stood for a moment staring up at these wonders. In all her years, the night sky never failed to fill her with awe.

Remembering her task, Ch'idzigyaak grabbed the upper rims of the caribou skins, laid them on the ground and briskly brushed off the crystal frost. After putting the skins up again, she went back inside to build up the campfire. Soon moisture dripped from the skin wall, which quickly dried.

Ch'idzigyaak shuddered to think of the melting frost dripping on them in the cold weather. How had they managed before? Ah, yes! The younger ones were always there, piling wood on the fire, peering into the shelter to make sure that their elders' fire did not go out. What a pampered pair they had been! How would they survive now?

Ch'idzigyaak sighed deeply, trying not to dwell on those dark thoughts, and concentrated instead on tending the fire without waking her sleeping companion. The shelter warmed as the fire crackled, spitting tiny sparks from the dry wood. Slowly, Sa' awoke to this sound and lay on her back for a long time before becoming aware of her friend's movement. Turning her aching neck slowly she began to smile but stopped as she saw her friend's forlorn look. In a pained grimace Sa' propped

herself up carefully on one elbow and tried to smile encouragingly as she said, "I thought yesterday had only been a dream when I awoke to your warm fire."

Ch'idzigyaak managed a slight smile at the obvious attempt to lift her spirits but continued to stare dully into the fire. "I sit and worry," she said after a long silence. "I fear what lies ahead, No! Don't say anything!" She held up her hands as her friend opened her mouth to speak.

"I know that you are sure of our survival. You are younger." She could not help but smile bitterly at her remark, for just yesterday they both had been judged too old to live with the young. "It has been a long time since I have been on my own. There has always been someone there to take care of me, and now..." She broke off with a hoarse whisper as tears fell, much to her shame.

Her friend let her cry. As the tears eased and the older woman wiped her dampened face, she laughed. "Forgive me, my friend. I am older than you. Yet I cry like a baby."

"We are like babies," Sa' responded. The older woman looked up in surprise at such an admission. "We are like helpless babies." A smile twitched her lips as her friend started to look slightly affronted by the remark, but before Ch'idzigyaak could take it in the wrong way Sa' went on. "We have learned much during our long lives. Yet there we were in our old age, thinking that we had done our share in life. So we stopped, just like that. No more working like we used to, even though our bodies are still healthy enough to do a little more than we ex-

pect of ourselves."

Ch'idzigyaak sat listening, alert to her friend's sudden revelation as to why the younger ones thought it best to leave them behind. "Two old women. They complain, never satisfied. We talk of no food, and of how good it was in our days when it really was no better. We think that we are so old. Now, because we have spent so many years convincing the younger people that we are helpless, they believe that we are no longer of use to this world."

Seeing tears fill her friend's eyes at the finality of her words, Sa' continued in a voice heavy with feeling. "We are going to prove them wrong! The People. And death!" She shook her head, motioning into the air. "Yes, it awaits us, this death. Ready to grab us the moment we show our weak spots. I fear this kind of death, more than any suffering you and I will go through. If we are going to die anyway, let us die trying!"

Ch'idzigyaak stared for a long time at her friend and knew that what she said was true, that death surely would come if they did not try to survive. She was not convinced that the two of them were strong enough to make it through the harsh season, but the passion in her friend's voice made her feel a little better. So, instead of feeling sadness because there was nothing further they could say or do, she smiled. "I think we said this before and will probably say it many more times, but yes, let us die trying." And with a sense of strength filling her like she had not thought possible, Sa' returned the smile as she got up to prepare

for the long day ahead of them.

CHAPTER 3
Recalling Old Skills

That day the women went back in time to recall the skills and knowledge that they had been taught from early childhood.

They began by making snowshoes. Usually birchwood was collected during late spring and early summer, but today the young birch would have to do. They didn't have the correct tools, of course, but the women managed with what they had to split the wood into four farts each, which they boiled in their large birch containers. When the wood became soft, the women bent it roundish and pointed at the tips. Putting two of these half-rounded sides together, the women awkwardly drilled many little holes into both sides with their small pointed sewing awls. The work was hard, but despite their aching fingers the women continued until they finished the task. Earlier, they had soaked the babiche in water. Now they took the softened material, sliced it into thin strips, and wove it onto the snowshoes.

As the babiche hardened with a little help from the campfire, the women prepared leather bindings for their snowshoes.

When they finished, the women beamed with pride. Then they walked atop the snow with their slightly awkward but serviceable snow- shoes to check their rabbit snares and were further cheered to find they had caught another rabbit. The knowledge that a few days before The People had tried to snare rabbits in the area without success made the women feel almost superstitious about their good luck. They went back to the camp feeling lighthearted about all that had been accomplished.

That night the women talked about their plans. They agreed that they could not remain in the fall camp where they had been abandoned, for there were not enough animals on which to survive the long winter. They also were afraid that potential enemies might come upon them. Other bands were traveling, too, even in the cold winter, and the women did not want to be exposed to such dangers. They also began to fear their own people because of the broken trust. The two women decided they must move on, fearing that the cold weather would force people to do desperate things to survive, remembering the taboo stories handed down for generations about how some had turned into cannibals to survive.

The two women sat in the shelter, thinking about where to go. Suddenly Ch'idzigyaak burst out, "I know of a place!"

"Where?" Sa' asked in an excited voice.

"Do you remember the place where we fished long ago?

The creek where the fish were so abundant that we had to build many caches to dry them?"

The younger woman searched her memory for a moment, and vaguely the place came to mind. "Yes, I do remember. But why did we not ever return?" she asked. Ch'idzigyaak shrugged. She did not know either.

"Maybe The People forgot that place existed," she ventured.

Whatever the reason, the two women agreed that it would be a good place to go now and since it was a long distance, they should leave at once. The women yearned to be as far away as possible from this place of bad memories.

The following morning they packed. Their caribou skins served many purposes. That day, they served as pulling sleds. Taking the two skins off the tent frame, the women laid the skins flat with the fur facing the snow. They packed their possessions neatly in the skins and laced them tightly shut with long strips of babiche. They fastened long woven ropes of mooseskin leather onto the front of the skin sleds, and each woman tied a rope around her waist. With the fur of the caribou hides sliding lightly across the dry, deep snow and the women's snowshoes making the walking easier, the two women began their long journey.

Temperatures had dropped, and the cold air made the women's eyes sting. Time and time again, they had to warm their faces with their bare hands, and they continually wiped

tears from their irritated eyes. But their fur and skin clothing served them well, for cold as it was, their bodies remained
warm.

The women walked late into the night. They had not gone
too far, but both were bone-weary and felt as though they had
been walking forever. Deciding to camp, the women dug deep
pits in the snow and filled them with spruce boughs. Then they
built a small campfire, re-boiling the squirrel meat and drinking
its broth. They were so tired they soon fell asleep. This time
they did not moan or twitch but slept deep and soundlessly.

Morning arrived, and the women awoke to the deep cold
surrounding them while the sky above seemed like a bowl of
stars. But as the women tried to climb out of their pits, their
bodies would not move. Looking into each other's eyes, the
women realized they had pushed their bodies beyond their
physical endurance. Finally, the younger, more determined Sa'
managed to move. But the pain was so great that she let out
an agonized groan. Knowing this would happen to her, too,
Ch'idzigyaak lay still for awhile, gathering courage to withstand
the pain she knew would come. Finally, she, too, made her way
slowly and painfully out of the snow shelter, and the women
limped around the camp to loosen their stiff joints. After they
chewed on the remaining squirrel meat, they continued their
journey, slowly pulling their laden toboggans.

That day would be remembered as one of the longest and
hardest of the days to come. They stumbled numbly on, many

times falling down into the snow from sheer fatigue and old age. Yet they pushed on, almost in desperation, knowing that each step brought them nearer to their destination.

The distant sunlight that appeared for a short while each day peeped hazily through the ice fog that hung in the air. Now and again, blue skies could be seen, but mostly the women noticed only their own frosty breath coming in thick swirls. Freezing their lungs was another worry, and they took care not to work too hard in the cold and, if such work was unavoidable, they wore a protective covering over their faces. This could cause irritating side effects, such as frost buildup where the covering brushed against their faces. However, the women did not notice such minor discomforts compared with their aching limbs, stiff joints, and swollen feet. Sometimes even the heavy sleds seemed to serve a purpose by keeping the women from falling flat on their faces as they pulled onward with the ropes wrapped around their chests.

As the few hours of daylight slipped away, the women's eyes readjusted to the darkness that began to enfold them. But they knew that night had not yet arrived and that there was still time to move. When it became time to camp, the women found themselves on a large lake. They could see the outline of trees along the shore and they knew that the forest would be a better place to camp. But they were so exhausted they could go no farther. Again they dug a deep pit in the snow, and after snuggling down and covering themselves with their skin blankets they

were soon asleep. The thick skin and fur clothing held their body heat and protected them from the cold air. The snow pit was as warm as any shelter aboveground, so the women slept, mindless of freezing temperatures that made even the most ferocious northern animals seek shelter.

The next morning, Sa' awoke first. The long sleep and cold air cleared her mind considerably. With a twisting grimace she stuck her head out of the hole to look around. She saw the outline of trees on the shore and remembered how they had been too tired to complete their crossing of the lake.

She got up slowly, not wanting to disturb her friend's slumber and knowing that with a wrong move her stiffened body would lock up and refuse to go farther. A smile hovered around her lips as she thought of how she and her friend had complained loudly and often of their minor aches and pains a few days before, and of the walking sticks they had used until forgetting them at the camp the day before. Slowly stretching in the chilly air, she made a mental note to remind her friend of this when the right time came. They could laugh over the fact that for years they had carried those sticks around to help them walk better and now, somehow, they had managed many miles without them. Putting on her snowshoes, Sa' walked about to loosen the stiffness in her sore joints.

From within the snow pit, Ch'idzigyaak looked up at her more agile companion who slowly circled the shelter. Ch'idzigyaak was still tired and feeling miserable. But she knew

she must do her best to stand beside her friend through this hardship. She had lived long enough to know that if she gave up, her friend would give up, too. So she forced herself to move, but the pain that filled her body made her lie back down, and let out a deep sigh.

Sa' saw that Ch'idzigyaak was having a hard time, so she reached down to help her climb out of the pit. Together they grunted, struggling to move. Soon they were walking again, and kept right on going until they reached the edge of the lake. There, they built a fire and, after eating some of the rabbit meat they had carefully rationed, they returned for their sleds and resumed their journey.

The frozen lakes seemed endless. Struggling through the many spruce trees, willow thickets, and thorn patches that lay between the lakes wore the women out until they felt as if they had traveled many more miles than they had. Despite having to make many detours around obstacles, the women never completely lost their sense of direction. Sometimes, fatigue clouded their judgement, and they found themselves straying slightly off course or going in circles, but they soon found their way again. In vain, they hoped that the slough they sought would appear suddenly. Indeed, there were times when one of them would fantasize that they had reached their destination. But the constant reminders of the intense cold and aching bones brought them quickly back to reality.

On the fourth night, the women almost stumbled onto

the slough. Everything around them stood shrouded under silvery moonlight. Shadows stretched beneath the many trees and over the slough. The women stood on the bank for a few moments, resting as their eyes took in the beauty of that special night. Sa' marveled at the power the land held over people like herself, over the animals, and even over the trees. They all depended on the land, and if its rules were not obeyed, quick and unjudgemental death could fall upon the careless and unworthy. Ch'idzigyaak looked at her friend as Sa' sighed deeply. "What's the matter?" she asked.

Sa's face creased in a sad smile. "Nothing is wrong, my friend. We are on the right trail after all. I was thinking about how it used to be that the land was easy for me to live on, and now it seems not to want me. Perhaps it is just my aching joints that are making me complain."

Ch'idzigyaak laughed. "Perhaps it is because our bodies are just too old, or maybe we are out of shape. Maybe the time will come when we will spring across this land again." Sa' joined in the joke.

Such musings were meant only to lift their spirits and the women knew that their journey was not over, nor would their struggle for survival become easier. Although they had grown soft in their old age, Ch'idzigyaak and Sa' knew they would pay a high price of hard toil before the land yielded them any comforts.

The two women walked down the winding slough until

they came upon a large river. Even in times of cold weather, the swishing undercurrents of the river eroded the ice and made it thin and dangerous to walk on. The women realized this as they carefully inched their way across the quiet river, keeping their senses alert for the sound of cracking ice or any hint of steam rising from between the ice chinks.

When they finally reached the other side, the tension and fatigue left both women mentally and physically drained. With what little energy remained, they numbly set to the task of building yet another overnight shelter.

CHAPTER 4

A Painful Journey

Nights past when they had managed to build shelters were nothing compared to this one, for the women were so tired they could barely move. In blind determination they stumbled about gathering spruce boughs for their beds and large chunks of wood for the campfire. Finally, they huddled together and stared as if hypnotized into the large orange blaze they ignited from the live coals carried from the first campsite. Soon they slipped mindlessly off to sleep. They did not hear the lonesome howl of a distant wolf, and before they knew it the cold air of morning brought them back to their senses.

They had fallen asleep leaning against one another and somehow managed to stay in that position all night. Because they were sitting up on their legs, the women knew getting up would not be easy. They sat still for a long time. Then Sa' made an effort to rise, but her legs had lost their feeling. She grunted and tried again. Meanwhile, Ch'idzigyaak closed her eyes tight-

ly and pretended to be asleep. She did not want to face the day.

Sa' gathered a little courage to force herself to move, but the aches in her bones proved to be too much for her this time. Again they had pushed their bodies beyond their limits. Without meaning to, Sa' let out a painful moan, and she felt a great urge to cry. She hung her head, defeated by all they had been through these past few days, and the cold made her feel even more despair. As much as she wanted to, her body would not move. She was too stiff.

Ch'idzigyaak listened lethargically to her friend's sniffles. She was amazed that she could sit and listen to Sa' cry and feel no emotion. Perhaps it was not meant for them to go on. Perhaps the young ones were right — she and Sa' were fighting the inevitable. It would be easy for them to snuggle deeper into the warmth of their fur clothing and fall asleep. They would not have to prove anything to anyone anymore. Perhaps the sleep that Sa' feared would not be so bad after all. At least, Ch'idzigyaak thought to herself, it would not be as bad as this.

Yet, for as little will as her older friend had, Sa' possessed enough determination for both of them. Shrugging off the cold, the pain in her sides, her empty stomach, and the numbness in her legs) she struggled to get up and this time succeeded. As had become her morning habit, she limped around the campsite until feeling slowly began to course through her bloodstream. When the circulation returned, there was more pain. But Sa' concentrated her attention on gathering more wood to build

the fire. Then she boiled a rabbit head to make a tasty broth, Ch'idzigyaak watched all this from between narrowed lids. She did not want her friend to know that she was awake, for then, Ch'idzigyaak felt, she would be obligated to move, and she did not want to move. Not now and not ever. She would stay exactly as she was, and perhaps death would steal her quickly away from the suffering. But her body was not ready to give in just yet. Instead of slipping blissfully into oblivion, Ch'idzigyaak suddenly felt the urgent need to relieve her bladder. She tried to ignore this, but soon her bladder could wait no more, and with a loud grunt she felt her bladder letting go. In quick panic she jumped up and headed for the willows, startling her friend. When Ch'idzigyaak came out of the willows looking slightly guilty, Sa' tilted her head in wonder. "Is something wrong?" she asked. Ch'idzigyaak, feeling embarrassed, admitted, "I surprised myself by how fast I moved. I did not think I would be able to move at all!"

Sa' was thinking of the day ahead. "After we have eaten, we should try to move on, even if we go only a little way today," she said. "Each step brings us closer to where we are going. Although I do not feel good today, my mind has power over my body, and it wants us to move on instead of staying here to rest — which is what I want to do." Ch'idzigyaak listened as she ate her portion of the rabbit head and broth. She, too, felt like staying there for a while. In fact, she desperately wanted to stay. But after putting aside her foolish thoughts, she felt ashamed and

reluctantly agreed they should move on.

Sa' felt a slight disappointment when Ch'idzigyaak agreed to resume their journey, wondering if deep within her she had hoped Ch'idzigyaak would refuse to move. But it was too late for second thoughts. So both women tied the ropes around their thin waists and pulled onward. As they walked, they kept their eyes open for signs of animals, for their food was nearly gone, and meat was their prime source of energy. Without it, their struggle would be over soon. Sometimes, the women stopped to discuss the route they had chosen and to ask themselves if it was the correct way. But the river led in only one direction from the slough, so the women walked along the riverbank as they kept a lockout for the narrow creek that would lead them to a place remembered for its plentiful fish long ago.

The days dragged on as the women slowly pulled their sleds across the deep snow. On the sixth day, Sa', who had grown accustomed to staring dully only at the path ahead, happened to glance up. Across the river she saw the opening to the creek. "We are there," she said in a soft, breathless voice. Ch'idzigyaak looked at her friend, then at the creek. "Except we are on the wrong side," she said. Sa' had to smile at her friend, who always seemed to find the negative side of a situation. Too tired to offer a lighter point of view, Sa' sighed to herself as she motioned to her friend to follow.

This time the two women did not worry about hidden cracks beneath the ice. They were too tired. Mindless of the

danger, they crossed the frozen river and kept right on going up the tributary. The women walked until late that night. The moon slowly emerged over the trees until it hovered above them, lighting their way along the narrow creek. Although they had walked more hours than they had on earlier days, the women continued on. They felt sure the old campsite was near and they wanted to reach their destination that night.

Just about the time Ch'idzigyaak was ready to beg her friend to stop, she saw the campsite. "Look over there!" she cried. "There are the fishracks we hung so long ago!" Sa' stopped and suddenly felt weak. It was with great effort that she stood on her shaking legs, for a feeling of somehow coming home suddenly overwhelmed her.

Ch'idzigyaak moved closer to her friend and gently placed an arm around her. They looked at each other and felt a surge of powerful emotion that left them speechless. They had traveled all this way by themselves. Good memories came back to them about the place where they had shared much happiness with friends and family. Now, because of an ugly twist of fate, they were here alone, betrayed by those same people. Because they were thrown together in hardship, the two women developed a sense of knowing what the other was thinking, and Sa' was usually the more sensitive one.

"It is better not to think of why we are here," she said. "We must set up our camp here tonight. Tomorrow we will talk." Clearing the bitter emotion from her throat, Ch'idzigyaak

heartily agreed. So, with slow, dragging movements, the two women climbed up the low bank of the creek and walked to the campsite, where they found an old tent frame that they used for shelter that night.

Though their clothing shielded them from the awful cold, the caribou skins did a better job. Coals from the fire pulsated amidst the ash all through the night and kept the shelter warm. Finally, the morning cold seeped through, and the women began to stir. Sa' was the first to move. This time her body did not protest so much as she moved about the shelter, placing the wood they had gathered the night before on the tiny embers still burning in the fireplace. After a few moments of softly blowing the dried sticks, a flame began a gentle dance as it spread onto the bundle of dry willows. Soon the shelter was warm and glowing.

That day, the women worked steadily, unmindful of their aching joints. They knew they would have to hurry to make final preparations for the worst of the winter, for even colder weather lay ahead. So they spent the day piling snow high around the shelter to insulate it and gathering all the loose wood they could find. Then without resting, they set a long line of rabbit snares, for the area was rich in willow, and there were many signs of rabbit life. Nighttime had arrived when the women made their way back to the camp. Sa' boiled the remains of the rabbits innards and the women feasted on the last of their food. After that, they leaned against their bedding and stared

into the campfire.

The two women had not known each other well before being abandoned. They had been two neighbors who thrived on each other's bad habit of complaining and on sharing conversations about things that did not matter. Now, their old age and their cruel fate were all they had in common. So it was that night, at the end of their painful journey together, they did not know how to converse in companionship, and instead, each woman dwelled on her own thoughts.

Ch'idzigyaak's mind went immediately to her daughter and grandson. She wondered if they were all right. A surge of hurt streaked through her as she thought about her daughter again. It was still hard for Ch'idzigyaak to believe that her own flesh and blood would refuse to come to her aid. As the self-pity overwhelmed her, Ch'idzigyaak fought the tears that threatened to spill from her eyes, and her lips formed a thin, rigid line. She would not cry! This was the time to be strong and to forget! But with that thought a huge single tear dripped down. She looked at Sa' and saw that she also was lost deep in thought. Ch'idzigyaak was perplexed by her friend. Except for a few moments of weakness, the woman next to her seemed strong and sure of herself, almost as if she were challenged by all of this. Curiosity replaced her pain and Sa' was startled when Ch'idzigyaak spoke.

"Once when I was a little girl, they left my grandmother behind. She could no longer walk and could hardly see. We

were so hungry that people were staggering around, and my mother whispered that she was afraid that people would think of eating people. I had not heard of any- thing like this before, but my family told stories of some who had grown desperate enough to do such things. My heart filled with fear as I clung to my mother's hand. If someone looked into my eyes, I would turn my head quickly, fearing he might take notice of me and consider eating me. That is how much fear I had. I was hun- gry, too, but somehow it didn't matter. Perhaps it was because I was so young and had my family all around me. When they talked about leaving my grandmother behind, I was horrified. I remember my father and brothers arguing with the rest of the men, but when my father came back to the shelter, I looked at his face and knew what would happen. Then I looked at my grand- mother. She was blind and too deaf to hear what was going on." Ch'idzigyaak took a deep breath before continuing with her story.

"When they bundled her up and put her blankets all around her, I think Grandmother sensed what was happening because as we began to leave the camp I could hear her crying." The older woman shuddered at the memory.

"Later, when I grew up, I learned that my brother and fa- ther went back to end my grandmother's life, for they did not want her to suffer. And they burned her body in case anyone thought of filling their bellies with her flesh. Somehow, we sur- vived that winter, though my only real memory of that time was

that it was not a happy one. I remember other times of empty stomachs, but none as bad as that one winter."

Sa' smiled sadly, understanding her friend's painful memories. She, too, remembered. "When I was young, I was like a boy," she began. "I was always with my brothers. I learned many things from them. Sometimes, my mother would try to make me sit still and sew, or learn that which I would have to know when I became a woman. But my father and brothers always rescued me. They liked me the way I was." She smiled at her memories.

"Our family was different from most. My father and mother let us do almost anything. We did chores like everyone else, but after they were done, we could explore. I never played with other children, only with my brothers. I am afraid I did not know what growing up was about because I was having so much fun. When my mother asked me if I had become a woman yet, I did not understand. I thought she meant in age, not in that way. And summer after summer, she would ask me the same question, and each time she looked more worried. I did not pay much attention to her. But as I grew as tall as my mother and just a little shorter than my brothers, people looked at me in a strange way. Girls younger than me already were with child and man. Yet I was still free like a child." Sa' laughed heartily as she now knew why she received all those strange looks from people then.

"I began to hear them laugh at me behind my back and I

became confused. In a way, I did not care what people thought about me, so I continued to hunt, fish, explore, and do what I pleased. My mother tried to make me stay home and work, but I rebelled. My brothers had taken women, and I told my mother she had plenty of help, and with that I would escape. When my mother turned to my father to discipline me, I would show up with a huge bundle of ducks, fish, or some other food, and my father would say, 'Leave her alone. 'Then I grew older, beyond that age when women should have man and child, and everyone was talking about me. I could not understand why, for although I was not with a man and having children, I was still doing my share of the work by providing food. There were times when I brought more food than the men. This did not seem to please them. About this time in my life, we experienced our worst winter. It was cold like this." Sa' motioned with her hand.

"Even babies died, and grown men began to panic, for as hard as they tried they could not find enough animals to eat. There was an old woman in our group whom I rarely noticed. The chief decided we had to move on in our search for food. There was a rumor that far away we would find caribou. This excited everyone.

"The old woman had to be carried. The chief did not want this burden, so he told every- one that we would leave her be-hind. No one argued, except me. My mother tried to stifle me, but I was young and unthinking. She told me that this was to be done for the sake of the whole group. She seemed like a cold,

unfeeling stranger as she tried to talk me out of my protest, but I angrily brushed her off. I was shocked and furious. I felt that The People were being lazy and were not thinking clearly. It was my job to talk some sense into them. And being who I was, I spoke up for the woman whom I hardly knew existed until then. I asked the men if they thought they were no better than the wolves who would shun their old and weak.

"The chief was a cruel man. I had avoided him until the day I stood before him and shouted angry words at his face. I could see that he was twice as angry as I was, but I could not stop myself. Even though I knew that the chief disliked me, I argued on, not listening to him as he tried to answer my accusations. His action was wrong, and I meant to make it right. As I continued to talk, I was unaware of the shock that awakened the group from its malnourished lethargy. A fearful look fell upon the chief's face and he put his large hand over my mouth. 'All right, strange young girl,' he said in a loud voice that I knew was meant to humiliate me. I could feel my chin go up farther so that he could see that I remained proud and unafraid. 'You will stay with the old one,' he said. I could hear my mother gasp, and my own heart sank. Yet I would not yield as I stared unblinkingly into his eyes.

"My family was deeply hurt, but pride and shame kept them from protesting. They did not want a daughter who would take such a stand against the strong leaders of the group. I did not think the leaders were strong. The chief acted as if I did not

exist after that, and I was ignored by everyone else except my family, who begged me to apologize to the leader. But I would not give in. My pride grew with each moment the others pretended I was not there, and I continued to plead for the old woman's life." Sa' broke into laughter at her impetuous youth.

"What happened after that?" Ch'idzigyaak wanted to know.

Sa' paused as she deeply inhaled the pain from those long-ago memories. Continuing in a subdued voice, she said, "After they left, I was not so brave. There were no animals to be found for miles around. But I was determined to show what could be done by my good intentions. So the old woman — I never did know her name, for I was too busy trying to keep us alive — and I ate mice, owls, and anything else that moved. I killed it, and we ate it. The woman died that winter. Then I was alone. Not even my pride and usual carefree ways could help me. I talked to myself all the time. Who else was there? They would think I was crazy if The People returned to find me talking to the air. At least you and I have each other," Sa' told her friend, who nodded in wholehearted agreement.

"Then I realized the importance of being with a large group. The body needs food, but the mind needs people. When the sun finally came hot and long on the land, I explored the country. One day as I was walking along, talking to myself as usual, someone said, 'Who are you talking to?' For a moment I thought I was hearing things. I stopped in my tracks and turned slowly to find a big, strong-looking man with his

arms crossed, smiling at me in a bold manner. Many feelings ran through me at that moment. I was surprised, embarrassed, and angry all at once. 'You scared me!' I said, trying to cover up my real feelings. Because my cheeks were burning, I knew I did not fool him, for his grin grew deeper. He asked me what I was doing out there alone, and I told him my story. I felt at that moment that I could trust him. He told me that the same thing happened to him. Only he was banished because he was foolish enough to fight over a woman who was meant for another man. We were together a long time before we became a man and woman together. I never saw my family again, and it was years later that we joined the band.

"Then he tried to fight with a bear and died. Foolish man," she added with grudging admiration, as a deep sadness weighed down her face.

It was the first time Ch'idzigyaak saw her friend so sad, and she broke the silence by saying, "You were luckier than I, for when it became apparent that I was not interested in taking a man, I was forced to live with a man much older than me. I hardly knew him. It was years before we had our child. He was older than I am now when he died."

Sa' laughed. "The People would have chosen a man for me too, had I been with them much longer." After a momentary silence, she continued. "Now here we are, truly old. I hear our bones creaking, and we are left behind to fend for ourselves." The women fell into silence as they struggled with their emo-

tions. They lay on their warm beds as the cold earth trembled outside. They thought about the experiences they had shared. As they fell into an exhausted sleep, each woman felt more at home because of her new knowledge of the other and because each had survived hard times before.

Days shortened as the sun sank deeper under the horizon. It grew so cold there were times when the women jumped as the trees around them cracked loudly from the cold pressure. Even the willows snapped. But as the women settled down they also became depressed. They feared the savage wolves that howled in the distance. Other imagined fears tormented them as well, for there was plenty of time to think as the dark days drifted slowly by. In what daylight they had, the two women forced themselves to move. They spent all their waking hours collecting firewood from underneath the deep snow. Though food was scarce, warmth was their main concern, and at night they would sit and talk, trying to keep each other from the loneliness and fears that threatened to overcome them. The People rarely spent precious time in idle conversation. When they did speak, it was to communicate rather than to socialize. But these women made an exception during the long evenings. They talked. And a sense of mutual respect developed as each learned of the others past hardships.

Many days went by before the women caught more rabbits. It had been some time since they had eaten a full meal. They managed to preserve their energy by boiling spruce boughs to

serve as a minty tea, but it made the stomach sour. Knowing it was dangerous to eat anything solid after such a diet, the two women first boiled the rabbit meat to make a nourishing broth, which they drank slowly. After a day of drinking the broth, the women cautiously ate one ham off a rabbit. As the days passed, they allowed themselves more portions, and soon their energy was restored.

With wood piled high around the shelter like a barricade, the women found that they had more time to forage for food. The hunting skills they learned in their youth reemerged, and each day the women would walk farther from the shelter to set their rabbit snares and to keep an eye out for any other animals small enough to kill. One of the rules they had been taught was that if you set snares for animals you must check them regularly. Neglecting your snareline brought bad luck. So, despite the cold and their own physical discomforts, the two women checked their snares each day and usually found a rabbit to reward them.

At nightfall, when their daily chores were completed, the women wove the rabbit fur into blankets and clothing, such as mittens and face coverings. Sometimes, to break the monotony, one would present a woven rabbit-far hat or mittens to the other. This always brought wide smiles.

As the days slowly passed, the weather lost its cold edge, and the women savored moments of glee — they had survived the winter! They regained what energy they had lost and now

they kept busy collecting more firewood, checking the rabbit snares and scouting the vast area for other animals. Though the women had lost the habit of complaining, they grew tired of the daily fare of rabbit meat and found themselves dreaming of other game to eat, such as willow grouse, tree squirrels, and beaver meat.

One morning, as Ch'idzigyaak awoke, she felt something was not quite right. Her heart pumped rapidly as she slowly got up, fearing the worst, and peeked out of the shelter. At first, all seemed still. Then suddenly she spotted a flock of willow grouse pecking at some tree debris that had fallen not far away. With trembling hands, she quietly got a long, thin strand of babiche out of her sewing bag and slowly crept out of the tent. Selecting a long stick from the nearby woodpile, she fashioned a noose at the end and began to crawl toward the flock.

Nervously, the birds started to cluck as they became aware of the woman's presence. Knowing that the birds were about to take fight, Ch'idzigyaak stopped for a few minutes to give them time to calm down. They were not too far from her now, and she hoped that Sa' would not awake and make a noise that would scare away the birds. With knees aching and hands slightly trembling, Ch'idzigyaak slowly pushed the stick forward. Some grouse excitedly flew away to another patch of willows nearby, but she steadfastly ignored them as she continued to lift the stick slowly as the remaining birds walked about faster. Ch'idzigyaak concentrated on the grouse closest

to her. It made small movements towards the noose, its head nodding back to front. As the birds started noisily to run and fly off, Ch'idzigyaak shoved the noose forward until the bird's head slipped right into it. Then she jerked the stick upward as the bird squawked and twisted until it hung motionless. Standing up with the dead grouse in her hand, Ch'idzigyaak turned toward the tent to find her friend's face wreathed in smiles. Ch'idzigyaak smiled back.

Looking into the air, Ch'idzigyaak took note of a warmth in the air. "The weather gets better," Sa' said softly and the older woman's eyes widened in surprise. "I should have noticed. Had it been cold, I would have frozen in my position of a sneaky fox." The women found great laughter in this as they went back into the shelter to prepare the meat of a different season to come. After that morning, the weather fluctuated between bitter cold and then warm and snowy days. That the women did not catch another bird failed to dampen their spirits, for the days gradually grew longer, warmer, and brighter.

CHAPTER 5

Saving a Cache of Fish

Soon winter was gone and the two old women spent more time hunting game. They feasted on the feisty little squirrels that bolted from tree to tree and on the flocks of willow grouse that seemed to be everywhere.

With the warm days of spring came the time for muskrat hunting. The women long ago had been tutored in the skills and patience required. First, special nets and traps had to be made. A willow branch was bent into a circle and bound securely at the ends. The women wove thin strips of moose leather into the frames until each formed a crude but sturdy net. Then, on a sunny day, they set out in search of a muskrat tunnel.

They walked a long way before they came to a cluster of lakes with signs of muskrat life. They picked out a lake with little black lumps of muskrat houses still showing on the rotting ice. After locating the muskrat tunnel, the women marked each end of the underground pathway with a stick. When the stick

moved, it meant a muskrat was coming through the tunnel and when it emerged from the opening, one of the women would snatch it with her net and end its life with a blow to the head. The first day, the women caught ten muskrats. But they were worn out by the stress of bending down and waiting, so the walk back to camp seemed long.

The spring days brought little time to talk or to reflect on the past as the women kept busy catching more muskrats and some beavers, all of which were smoke-dried for preservation. Their days were so full they hardly took time to eat, and at night they slept deeply. When they decided they had caught more than their share of muskrat and beaver, they packed everything and hauled it back to their main camp.

Still, the women felt vulnerable. The area was rich in animal life now, and they felt in time other people might come. Normally, other people meant their own kind. But since being left behind on that cold winter day, the women felt defenseless against the younger generation and had lost trust that they knew they never could regain. Now, suspicion left them wary of what might happen if anyone were to come upon them and find their growing store of food. They talked about what they should do, and in time they agreed they should move to a place less desirable — a place other people would not wish to explore, perhaps a place where it would be hard to manage the mighty swarms of summer insects.

The women did not relish having to face the many blood-

thirsty mosquitoes that awaited them in the thick willow bushes and trees. But their fear of people was greater. So they packed all they had and began the unpleasant trek to the hiding place. They decided to work in the heat of the day when mosquitoes seemed to hide. At night, they sat near a smoky fire to protect themselves. It took days to transfer the camp, but at last, the women stood by the creek and took one last look around, wishing a wind would blow away any hints of their presence.

Before deciding to move, the women had torn large amounts of birch bark from the trees. Now they recognized their mistake. Although by habit they took pieces of bark from trees spaced far apart, the women knew that any alert eye would take notice of this detail. But they also knew that nothing could be done about it, and in resignation they left the camp for their less desirable place within the thickets.

The two women spent the remaining days of spring trying to make their new camp more hospitable. They put up their shelters under the deep shade of tall spruce trees and hidden among many willows. Then they found a cool spot where they dug a deep hole that they lined with willows. There, they laid their large cache of dried, meat for the summer. They also placed a few traps atop the ground to scare off any sharp-nosed predators. The mosquitoes were everywhere, and as they worked, the women relied on long-used methods of shielding themselves to keep from being eaten alive. They hung leather tassles around their faces and their thick clothing to keep the

small insects from biting into their skin. When it seemed as if they would be carried away, the women covered their skin with muskrat grease to repel the masses of flying pests. Meanwhile, they charted a small hidden path to the creek where they got their water and, with summer nearly upon them, made their fish traps. Once the traps were set, the women had no trouble catching fish and found they had to move nearer to the creek to keep up with the task of cutting and drying. In time, a bear began helping himself to the fish the women had stored. This worried them, but in time they reached an unusual agreement with the bear. They carried the fish guts far from the camp where the greedy bear could laze about and eat at his leisure.

Too soon, the sun lay orange and cool on the evening horizon, and the women knew summer was dwindling. About this time, the spawning salmon began to find their way up the little creek, much to the women's pleasure, and for a short while they were busy with the reddish fish meat. The bear disappeared from the area, but still the women disposed of fish innards far down the creek. If the bear did not eat them, the ever present ravens would devour them soon enough. The women also were frugal, and they preserved many inside parts of the fish for other uses. For instance, the salmon intestines could be used for containing water, and the skin was fashioned into round bags to hold dried fish. These tasks kept them so busy they were up from early morning until late at night, and before they knew it, the short Arctic summer passed, and fall crept upon them.

When the season changed, the women retired from fishing and hauled their large supply back to the hidden camp. There they found a new problem. They had collected so much fish that there was no place to store it, and with the approaching winter there was no shortage of small animals searching for winter food. Eventually, the women made standing caches for their fish, and they placed great bundles of thorns and brush beneath them to discourage animals from bothering the fish. Perhaps this method worked, or perhaps it was just their luck, but animals kept away from their caches.

Far behind the camp was a low hill that the women had not had time to explore. One day, with their summer hunting finished, Sa' found herself wondering what bounties might lie on that hill or around it. So she took her spear and bow and the arrows the women had made, announcing that she would visit the hill. Ch'idzigyaak did not approve but could see that her friend would not be deterred.

"Just keep the fire going, and your spear nearby, and you should be safe," Sa' said as she set out, leaving Ch'idzigyaak behind shaking her heard in disapproval.

It was a day of abandon for Sa'. She felt light-hearted for the first time in more years than she could remember, and like a child, she grasped greedily at the feeling. The day was beautiful. The leaves were turning a brilliant gold and the air was crisp and clear as Sa' all but skipped along an animal trail. From a distance, one would not be able to see that Sa' was an older

woman, for she looked lithe and energetic. When she reached the top, she gasped in surprise. Before her lay vast patches of cranberries, Sa' dropped to her knees and began to scoop handfuls of the small red fruit, stuffing them into her mouth. As she gorged on this delicious food, a movement in the nearby brush made her freeze instantly.

Slowly, Sa' forced herself to look toward the sound, imagining the worst. She relaxed when she saw that it was only a bull moose. Then she remembered that this time of year a bull moose could be the most fearful animal on four legs. Usually timid, the bull moose in his rutting stage was no longer afraid of man or of anything else that moved or stood in his way.

The moose remained still for a long time as if he were just as surprised and undecided about the small woman who stood before him as she had been about him. As her pulse slowed almost to normal, Sa' imagined the delectable taste of moosemeat during the long winter months ahead. In another moment of unthinking craziness, she reached for an arrow from her pack and placed it in her bow. The moose's ears flipped forward at the movement, then it turned and ran in the opposite direction just as the arrow landed harmlessly on the soft ground.

Pressing her fate, Sa' followed. She could not run as strongly as when she was young, but with something that looked more like a limp than a jog, Sa' was able to pursue the large animal. A moose can outrun a human any time unless, of course, there is too much snow. But on a snowless day like this,

the moose sprinted far ahead as Sa', gasping for breath, barely caught a glimpse of his large hind-end disappearing behind the brush. The big bull stopped many times, almost as if he were playing a game with Sa', and just when she almost caught up, he would saunter far ahead once more. Normally, a moose will run as far as he can from any predator. But today, the moose did not feel much like running, nor did he feel threatened, so the old woman was able to keep him in sight. She was stubborn and would not give up, although she knew that she was outmatched. By late afternoon, the moose seemed to grow tired of the game as he watched her from the corner of his dark round eyes, and with one flip of his ear he began to run faster. Only then did Sa' admit to herself that there was no way she could catch it. She stared at the empty brush in defeat. Slowly she turned back, thinking to herself, "If only I were forty years younger, I might have caught him."

It was late that night when Sa' returned to the camp where her friend kept watch by a large campfire. As Sa' sank wearily into a bundle of spruce boughs, Ch'idzigyaak could not help but blurt out, "I think many more years were taken from me while I worried for you." Despite the admonishment in her voice, Ch'idzigyaak was deeply relieved that no harm had come to her friend.

Knowing that she had been foolish, Sa' understood what her friend had been through and she felt ashamed. Ch'idzigyaak handed her a bowl of warm fish meat and Sa' ate slowly. When

a little of her strength returned, Sa' told Ch'idzigyaak how she spent the day. Ch'idzigyaak smiled as she envisioned her friend chasing the long-legged bull, but she did not smile too broadly for it was not in her nature to laugh at others. Sa' was grateful for that, and then, remembering the cranberries, told her friend about the great find and they both were cheered.

It took a few days for Sa' to recover from her adventure with the moose, so the two old women sat still and wove birch bark into large round bowls. Then they went back to the hill and gathered as many berries as they could carry. By that time, autumn was upon them and the nights became chillier, reminding the women that there was no time to waste in gathering their winter wood supply.

They piled wood high around their cache and shelter, and when they cleared all the wood from the area around the camp, they walked far back into the forest, packing in more bundles of wood on their backs. This went on until snowflakes fell from the sky, and one day the women awoke to a land shrouded in white. Now that winter was near, the women spent more time inside their shelter by the warm fire. Their days seemed easier now that they were prepared. Soon the women fell into a daily routine of collecting wood, checking rabbit snares, and melting snow for water. They sat evenings by the campfire, keeping each other company. During the months past, the women were too busy to think about what had happened to them, and if the thought did cross their minds, they blocked it out. But now

that they had nothing else to do in the evenings, those unwelcome thoughts kept coming back until soon each woman began to talk less as each stared thoughtfully into the small fire. They felt it was a taboo to think of those who had abandoned them, but now the treacherous thoughts invaded their minds.

The darkness grew longer, and the land became silent and still. It took much concentration for the two women to fill their long days with work. They made many articles of rabbit-fur clothing such as mittens, hats, and face coverings. Yet, despite this, they felt a great loneliness slowly enclose them.

CHAPTER 6

Sadness among The People

The chief stood surveying his surroundings with eyes made a little older by deep sadness. His people were in a desperate state, their eyes and cheeks sunk low in gaunt faces and their tattered clothing barely able to keep out the freezing cold. Many of them were frostbitten. Luck had gone against them. In desperation, still searching for game, they had returned to the place where they abandoned the two old women the winter before.

Sadly, the chief remembered how he fought the urge to turn back and save the old ones. But taking them back into the band would have been the worst thing for him to do. Many of the more ambitious younger men would have seen this as an act of weakness. And the way things had been going, The People would have been easily convinced that their leader was not dependable. No, the chief had known that a drastic change in leadership would have proved more damaging than the hunger,

for in times when a band is starving, bad politics lead only to further disaster. The chief remembered that moment of terrible weakness when he had almost allowed his emotions to ruin them all.

Now, once more, The People were suffering, and this winter found them on the verge of hopelessness. After turning their backs on the old women, The People traveled many hard miles before coming on a small herd of caribou. The meat sustained them until spring when they began to harvest fish, ducks, muskrats, and beaver. But just when they regained their energy to hunt and dry their food, the summer season ended, and it was time to think of moving toward the place where they would be able to find winter meat. The chief had never known such terrible luck. As they traveled, the fall season came and went, and once more the band found itself nearly out of food. Now the chief looked at The People wearily with a feeling of panic and self-doubt. How long could he hold out before he, too, became lost in the hunger and fatigue that undermined his decisions? The People seemed to have given up trying to survive. They no longer cared to hear his lectures, staring at him with dulled eyes as if he made no sense.

Something else that troubled the chief was his decision to return to the place where they had left the old women. No one argued as he led them here, but the chief knew they were surprised. Now they stood looking around as if they expected something from him, or expected to see the two women. The

chief avoided their eyes, not wanting them to know that he was as confused as they were. There was not a single sign that anyone had been left here. Not one bone gave evidence that the old ones had died. Even if an animal had stripped their bones of flesh, surely something would have been left behind to show that humans had died here. But there was nothing, not even the tent that had sheltered the women.

Among The People was a guide named Daagoo. He was an old man, younger than the two old women, but still considered an elder. In his younger days, Daagoo had been a tracker, but the years had dimmed his vision and skills. He observed out loud what none of the others would acknowledge. "Maybe they moved on," he said in a low voice so that only the chief would hear him. But in the silence, many heard him and some felt a surge of hope for the women many had loved.

After setting up camp, the chief summoned the guide and three of his strongest young hunters. "I do not know what is going on, but I have a feeling that all is not as it appears to be. I want you to go to the camps near here and see what you can find."

The chief was quiet about what he suspected, but he knew that the guide and the three hunters would understand, especially Daagoo, for he had watched the chief from season to season and had come to know what the man was thinking. Daagoo respected the chief and realized that he suffered from self-loathing because of the part he had played in abandoning the old

women. The guide knew the chief despised his own weakness, for it showed in the hard lines of bitterness etched on his face. The old man sighed. He knew that soon the self-hate would take its toll, and he did not like the thought of a good man such as the chief being destroyed this way. Yes, he would try to find out what had happened to the women, even if the effort was wasted.

Long after the four men left camp the chief stared after them. He could not find a definite reason why he wasted precious energy and time on what might be a futile effort. Yet he, too, had a strange feeling of hope. Hope for what? He had no answer. All the chief knew for sure was that in hard times The People should hold together, and last winter they had not done so. They had inflicted an injustice on themselves and the two old women, and he knew that The People had suffered silently since that day. It would be good if the two women survived, but the chief knew the odds weighed against that hope. How could two feeble ones survive freezing cold without food or the strength to hunt? The chief acknowledged this, yet he could not still the small speck of hope that sprang from months of hardship. Finding the women alive would give The People a second chance and that, perhaps, was what he hoped for most.

Each of the four men was conditioned to run long distances. What took the two women days to travel to the first camp the year before took the four men a single day. They found nothing but endless snow and trees. The trek taxed their limited energy, and they decided to spend the night there. When

the first hint of morning dawned, the men were up and jogging once more.

Daylight was fading when the men arrived at the second camp, and the younger men saw no evidence that it had been used in a long time. Impatience began to overtake them. They had been trained from childhood to respect their elders, but sometimes they thought they knew more than the older ones. Although they did not say so out loud, they felt precious time was being wasted when they should be hunting for moose.

"Let's turn back now," one of the young me suggested, and the others agreed quickly.

The guide's eyes lit up in amusement. How impatient they were! Yet Daagoo did not criticize the others for he, too, had been impatient as a young man. Instead, he said, "Take a closer look around you." The young hunters looked at him impatiently.

"Look closely at those birch trees," Daagoo insisted, and the men stared blankly at the trees. They saw nothing unusual. Daagoo sighed, and this caught the attention of one of the younger men, who tried again to see what the old man saw. Finally, his eyes widened. "Look!" he said, pointing to an empty patch on a birch tree. Then they saw that other trees spaced widely throughout the area had been stripped carefully, almost as if done intentionally so that no one would notice.

"Maybe it was another band," one of the men said.

"VVhy would they try to hide those empty spots on the trees?" Daagoo asked. The young man shrugged, unable to find

an answer.

Then Daagoo gave them instructions. "Before we return," he said, "I want to search this area." Before they could protest, the guide pointed them off in different directions. "If you see anything unusual, come right back here and we will go together to see what it is. "Tired as they were, the men began their search, although they were sulky and did not believe that the two women still lived.

Meanwhile, Daagoo set out in the direction he believed the two old women might have taken. "If I were afraid to be found by The People who left me to die, I would go this way, "he muttered to himself. "It is a senseless direction because it is far from water. But in winter they would not have to rely on the river, so I think they might be this way."

Daagoo walked a long distance into the willows and beneath the tall spruce trees. As he trudged farther and farther over the snow, he felt weary and wondered if he was doing the right thing. How was it possible to believe that two old women could survive when they, The People, barely made it through that winter? Especially those two women. All they did was complain. Even when little children were hungry, the women complained and criticized. Many times, Daagoo expected someone to silence them, but that had not happened until the day things had gotten out of control. Daagoo began to feel they were on a useless hunt. The two women must have gotten lost and died along the way. Perhaps they had tried to cross the river

and drowned.

As Daagoo thought about all of this, he became more doubtful with each negative thought. Then, suddenly, he smelled something. In the crystal-clear winter air, a light scent of smoke drifted past his nose and was gone. Daagoo stood very still as he tried to catch the scent once more, but there was nothing. For a moment, he wondered if it had been his imagination. Perhaps a summer fire nearby had left its lingering smell in the air. Not wanting to believe that, the old man backtracked slowly until once again he caught the scent. It was a light smell, but this time Daagoo knew that it was no remnant of a summer fire. No, this smoke had a freshness about it. Excited, he tried walking first in one direction, then another until the smoke grew stronger. Convinced that it came from a campfire nearby, his face crinkled into a broad grin as a certainty filled him — the two women had survived.

Daagoo hurried back to get the young men who were waiting as impatiently as before. They did not want to follow when he beckoned, but reluctantly, they followed Daagoo into the night for what seemed a long time. Finally, the guide held out his hand signaling them to stop. Lifting his nose, he told them to smell the air. The hunters sniffed but did not smell anything. "What is it you want us to smell?" one of them asked.

"Just keep smelling," Daagoo answered, so the men sniffed the air again until one exclaimed, "I smell smoke!" The others walked around sniffing the air with more interest now until

they, too, smelled it. Still skeptical, one of the younger men asked Daagoo what he expected to find. "We will see," he said simply as he led them farther toward the smoke.

The guides eyes strained into the darkness looking for the light of a campfire. He saw nothing but outlines of spruce trees and willows. Aided by the small lights of the many stars above, Daagoo saw that the snow was untrampled. Everything was still and quiet. Yet, the evidence of smoke told him that somewhere near someone was camping. As sure as the blood raced through his veins, the old tracker was now confident that the two old women were alive and at that moment, close. He could not contain his excitement, turning to the younger men and saying, "The two old women are near."

Chills ran down the spines of the younger men. They still did not believe that the old ones had survived.

Cupping his hands to his mouth, Daagoo called the women's names into the velvet night and identified himself. Then he waited, hearing only the sound of his own words swallowed by the silence.

CHAPTER 7

The Stillness is Broken

Ch'idzigyaak and Sa' had settled down for the night. As usual, after doing their daily chores and eating their supper, the two women sat and talked over their fire. They spoke more of The People these days. Loneliness and time had healed their most bitter memories, and the hate and fear born from last year's unexpected betrayal seemed to have been numbed by the many nights they spent sitting and listening to their own thoughts. It all seemed like a distant dream. Now, with their bellies full, the women found themselves in the comfort of their shelter speaking of how much they missed The People. When they ran out of conversation, the women sat silently, each wrapped in her own thoughts.

Suddenly, out of the stillness, the women heard their names called. From across the campfire, their eyes met, and they knew what they heard was not their imagination. The man's voice became loud, and he identified himself. The wom-

en knew the old guide. Perhaps they could trust him. But what of the others? It was Ch'idzigyaakwho spoke first. "Even if we do not answer, they will find us."

Sa' agreed. "Yes, they will find us," she said as her mind raced with many thoughts.

"What will we do?" Ch'idzigyaak whined in panic.

Sa' took a while to think. Then she said, "We must let them know we are here." Seeing the look of hysteria enter her friend's eyes, Sa' hastened to say in smooth, confident tones, "We must be brave and face them. But my friend, be prepared for anything." She waited a moment before she added, "Even death." This did not comfort Ch'idzigyaak, who looked as frightened as her friend ever had seen her.

The two women sat a long time trying to gather what courage they had left. They knew they could run no longer. Finally, Sa' got up slowly and went outside into the cold night air, hollering rather hoarsely, "We are here!"

Daagoo had been standing patiently, alertly, while the young hunters eyed him in doubt. What if it were someone else? An enemy perhaps? Just as one of the men was about to voice doubts, out of the darkness they heard Sa' answer. The old guide's face broke into a wide smile. He knew it! They were alive. Immediately, they headed in the direction of the sound. The cold air made the woman's voice seem close, but it took the men some time to reach the camp.

Finally, the men approached the light of the campfire that

had been built outside the shelter. Standing by it were the two old women armed with long, sharp, dangerous-looking spears. Daagoo had to smile in admiration of the old women who stood like two warriors ready to defend themselves. "We mean you no harm," he assured them.

The women stared at him defiantly a moment before Sa' said, "I believe you come in peace. But why are you here?" The guide stood a moment, unsure how to explain himself. "The chief sent me here to find you. He believed you were alive and told us to find you."

"Why?" Ch'idzigyaak asked suspiciously.

"I do not know," Daagoo said simply. Indeed, he was surprised to find that he did not know what he or the chief thought would happen once they found the two women, for it was obvious that the women did not trust him or the other men. "I will have to return to the chief to report that we have found you," he said. The two women knew this. "What then?" Sa' asked.

The guide shrugged. "I do not know. But the chief will protect you no matter what happens."

"Like he did the last time?" Ch'idzigyaak asked sharply.

Daagoo knew that if he wanted to, he and the three hunters easily could overtake these two women and their weapons. Yet, he felt his admiration grow stronger because the two women were ready to fight whatever they had to face. These were not the same women he had known before.

"You have my word," he said quietly, and the women could

feel the magnitude of what he said as they stood still a long time.

Sa' noticed how worn and weary the men looked. Even the guide who stood proudly had a destitute look about him. "You look tired," she said in a grudging tone. "Come inside," and she led them into their spacious and warm shelter.

The four men entered the tent cautiously, knowing that they were not welcome guests. The women motioned them to sit down, and after the men were seated around the warm fire, Sa' dug around in the back of her bedding along the tent wall and pulled out a fish bag, handing a portion of dried fish to each of the men. As the men ate the fish, they looked around. They could see that the women's bedding was made of newly woven rabbit fur. The two women looked to be in better shape than The People. How could that be? After the men ate their dried fish, Sa' served them boiled rabbit broth, which they drank gratefully.

Meanwhile, Ch'idzigyaak sat to the side staring rather balefully at the hunters, making them feel uncomfortable. With astonishment, the men realized these two women not only had survived but also sat before them in good health while they, the strongest men of the band, were half starved.

Sa' also stared at the men as they ate their food. She noticed that they tried to eat slowly, but now that they were in the light, she could tell from their lean faces that they had not been eating well. Ch'idzigyaak noticed this, too, but her heart was

filled with resentment at this unwanted intrusion, and she did not feel pity. When the men finished their food, Daagoo looked at the women expectantly as he waited for them to say something.

For a while no one broke the silence. Finally, Daagoo said, "The chief believed that you survived, so he sent us to find you." Ch'idzigyaak let out an angry grunt, and when the men turned to her, she gave them a mean look and turned her face away. She could not believe that these people had the nerve to search for them. Surely Sa' could see that they were up to no good. Sa' reached out and patted her friend's hand consolingly, then turned to the men and said simply, "Yes, we have survived."

Daagoo's mouth twitched in amusement at Ch'idzigyaak's wrath. Yet Sa' seemed not to hold too much of a grudge, so he avoided the glaring eyes of Ch'idzigyaak and spoke to Sa' instead. "We are starving, and the cold gets worse. Again we have little food, and we are in the same shape as when we left you. But when the chief hears you are well, he will ask you to come back to our group. The chief and most of The People feel as I do. We are sorry for what was done to you."

The women sat silently a long time. Finally Sa' said, "So you may leave us alone once more just when we need you the most?" Daagoo took a few minutes to respond, wishing the chief was there to answer, for the chief was more experienced in answering such questions.

"I cannot say that it will not happen again. In hard times,

some grow meaner than wolves, and others grow scared and weak, like I did when you were left behind." Daagoo's voice filled with sudden emotion at those last words, but he steadied his voice and continued. "I can tell you one thing right now. If it ever does happen again, I will protect you with my own life as long as I live." As he spoke, Daagoo realized that in these two women, whom he once thought of as helpless and weak, he had rediscovered the inner strength that had deserted him the winter before. Now, somehow, he knew that he never would believe himself to be old and weak again.

Never!

The younger men had sat quietly and listened to the exchange between their elders. Now, one of them spoke out in a youthfully passionate voice, "I, too, will protect you if anyone ever tries to do you harm again." Everyone looked at him in surprise. Then his peers also vowed to protect the two women, for they had been witness to a miraculous survival and had regained a stronger sense of respect for the old ones. The women could feel their hearts soften at these words. Still, there was distrust, for, though they believed these men, the women were unsure about the others.

The two women huddled together for a private conference. "Can we trust them?" Ch'idzigyaak asked. Sa' paused a moment, then nodded her head and said softly, "Yes."

"What of the other people? What if they knew of our caches? Do you think they will hold back when they see all our food?

Look how hungry these men are. Last year they did not respect us. Here you are willing to let them come to us! My friend, I fear that they will take our food from us whether we like it or not," Ch'idzigyaak said. Sa' already had thought of this, but she was not afraid. Instead, she answered, "We have to remember that they are suffering. Yes, they were too quick to condemn us, but now we have proven them wrong. If they do the same thing, we both know that we can survive. We have proven that much to ourselves.Now we must put aside our pride long enough to remember that they are suffering. If not for the adults, then for the children. Could you forget your own grandson?"

Ch'idzigyaak knew her friend was right, as usual. No, she could not be so selfish as to let her grandson go hungry when she had so much food to eat. The men waited patiently as the two women whispered between themselves.

Sa' was not through talking, for she knew that Ch'idzigyaak still harbored fear about what was happening and needed confidence to face the future. "They do not know we have done well for ourselves," she said. "But tomorrow in the daylight they will see, and then we will know if what they say is true. But remember this, my friend. If they do the same to us again, we will survive. And if they truly mean what they say, then maybe we will always be a reminder to them in harder times ahead."

Ch'idzigyaak nodded in agreement. For a moment, seeing these members of the band, she felt her old fears and forgot her renewed strength.She looked at her friend with great fondness.

Sa' always seemed to know the right thing to say.

In the shelter that night, the two women and the guide exchanged stories while the younger men sat in respectful and attentive silence. The old man told all that had happened after The People left the two women behind. He spoke of the ones who had died. Most were children. Unshed tears glistened in the old women's eyes as they listened, for they had loved some of these people, and the children were among their favorites. The women could not bear to think of how much the children might have suffered before they died so young and so cruelly.

After Daagoo finished his story, Sa' told him how they survived. The men sat with mixed emotions. The story she told sounded unbelievable, yet the women's very presence was evidence of its truth. Sa' did not mind the look of awe she saw in the men's faces. She continued telling her story as she looked back into the eventful year she and Ch'idzigyaak had shared. When she ended her story by telling them of their many food caches, their visitors' eyes became alert.

"When we heard your voice the first time, we knew we could trust you. We also knew that since you were able to find us in the night that it would take little time for you to find our food caches, too. That is why I am telling you now. We know you mean us no harm." Sa' spoke directly to Daagoo. "But what of The People? If they can do such a thing as leave us behind, then they will have no feelings about taking what is ours. They will think of us again as weak and old with no need for our large

caches. I do not blame them now for what they have done to us, for my friend and I know what hunger can do to a person. But we have worked hard for what we have, and though we knew it would be too much for us to eat during the winter, we stored it anyway. Maybe it was because we thought this might happen." Sa' paused to consider her words carefully. Then she added, "We will share with The People, but they must not become greedy and try to take our food, for we will fight to our deaths for what is ours."

The men sat in silence listening to Sa' speak in a strong and passionate voice. Then she laid down their terms: "You will stay at the old camp. We do not wish to see anyone else but you," Sa' motioned to Daagoo, and the chief. We will give you food, and we hope The People will eat sparingly in knowledge of harder times to come. This is all we can do for you." The guide nodded in acknowledgement and said in a quiet voice, "I will return with this message to the chief."

After they said all that had to be said, the women invited the men to sleep on one side of the shelter. For the first time in a long time, the women felt themselves relax. In those long months they feared many things. Now their visions of wolves and other predators faded away, and the women fell into a worry-free sleep.

They were no longer alone.

CHAPTER 8

A New Beginning

Before the men left the next day, the women packed large bundles of dry fish, enough to restore The People's energy for travel. Meanwhile, the chief waited anxiously. He feared that something had happened to his men, yet hope kept intruding on that thought. When the men returned, the chief quickly gathered the council to hear their story.

The guide told the stunned people what they had discovered. When he finished his story, he told them that the women did not trust them and did not want to see them. Daagoo told them of the terms the women had set. After a few minutes of silence, the chief said, "We will respect the women's wishes. Anyone who disagrees will have to fight me."

Daagoo was quick to join in, "The young men and I will stand by you." The council members who had suggested abandoning the two old women were deeply ashamed. Finally, one of them spoke. "We were wrong to leave them behind. They

proved it so. Now we will pay them back with respect."

After the chief announced the news to all, The People agreed to follow the rules set by the two women. After their energy was restored by the nourishing dried fish, The People began to pack, for they could not wait to see the two women. In this time of hardship the news of their survival filled the band with a sense of hope and awe. Ch'idzigyaaks daughter, Ozhii Nelii, wept when she heard the news. She had believed her mother to be dead but knew, despite her own overwhelming relief, that her mother would never forgive her. Shrub Zhuu was so ecstatic that, when he heard the news, the young boy immediately gathered his things and was ready to go.

It took the band quite a while to reach the camp where the bark had been stripped off the birch trees. The chief and Daagoo had gone ahead to meet with the two women, and when they arrived at the women's camp, the chief had to contain himself from embracing them. The women eyed him with distrust, so they all sat down to talk instead. The women told the chief what they expected from The People. He responded by telling them their wishes would be obeyed. "We will give you enough food for The People, and when it becomes low, we will give you more food. We will give you small portions at a time," Sa' told the chief, who nodded his head almost humbly.

It took another day before the band reached the new camp, unpacked and set up tents. Then the chief and his men arrived with bundles of fish and rabbit-fur clothing. Daagoo had hinted

boldly to the old women of the poor condition of the band's clothing after he spotted their large collection of rabbit-far garments. The women both knew they never would use the many mittens, head coverings, blankets and vests they had made in their spare time, so they felt obligated to share with those who needed them. After The People settled down in their new camp and their bellies no longer cried for nourishment, they became more curious about the two old women. But they were forbidden to go near that camp.

The colder days came and stayed a long time, and The People carefully rationed the food that the old women shared. Then the hunters killed a large moose and hauled it many miles back to the camp where all rejoiced at the good fortune.

All this time the chief and the guide took turns making daily visits to the women. When it became apparent that the two women also were curious about The People, the chief asked permission for others to visit, too. Ch'idzigyaakwas quick to say no, for her pride was the strongest. But later, the two women talked about it and admitted to themselves that they were ready for visitors. This was especially so for Ch'idzigyaak, who missed her family terribly. When the chief arrived the next day, the two women told him of their decision, and soon people began visiting. At first they were timid and unsure. But after a few visits, they all talked more easily, and soon laughter and light-hearted chatter could be heard from inside the shelter. Each time the visitors came, they brought the two women gifts of moosemeat

or animal furs, which the women accepted gratefully.

Relations became better between The People and the two women. Both learned that from hardship, a side of people emerged that they had not known. The People had thought themselves to be strong, yet they had been weak. And the two old ones whom they thought to be the most helpless and useless had proven themselves to be strong. Now, an unspoken understanding existed between them, and The People found themselves seeking out the company of the two women for advice and to learn new things. Now they realized that because the two women had lived so long, surely they knew a lot more than The People had believed.

Visitors came and went daily from the women's camp. Long after they left, Ch'idzigyaak would stand and stare after them. Sa' watched her and felt pity for her friend, for she knew that Ch'idzigyaak expected to see her daughter and grandson, but they did not come. Ch'idzigyaak harbored a secret fear in her heart that perhaps something bad had happened to them and The People did not want to tell her, but she was afraid to ask.

One day, as Ch'idzigyaak gathered wood, a young voice behind her said softly, "I have come for my hatchet," Ch'idzigyaak stood slowly and the wood in her arms fell unnoticed to the ground as she turned. They stared at each other, almost as if they were in a dream and could not believe what they saw. Faces wet with tears, Ch'idzigyaak and her grandson stared at each

other in happiness, and no words seemed worth speaking at that moment. Without further hesitation, Ch'idzigyaak reached out to embrace this young boy whom she loved.

Sa' stood by smiling at the happy reunion. The young boy looked up to see Sa' and went over to her and gave her a gentle hug. Sa' felt her heart swell with love and pride for this youngster.

Still, Ch'idzigyaak wondered about her daughter. Despite all that had happened, Ch'idzigyaak yearned to see her own flesh and blood. Being the observant one, Sa' knew this was why her friend seemed sad despite their good fortune. One day after another of the grandsons visits, Sa' reached over and grasped her friend's hand. "She will come," she said simply, and Ch'idzigyaak nodded her head, although she did not quite believe it.

Winter was almost over. A well-trodden path lay between the two camps. The People could not get enough of the women's company, especially the children, who spent many hours laughing and playing in the camp while the old women sat beside their shelter and watched. They were grateful to have survived to witness this. No longer did they take each day for granted.

The young grandson came every day. He helped his grandmothers with their daily chores as before and listened to their stories. One day, the older woman could wait no longer and finally found the courage to ask, "Where is my daughter? Why

does she not come?" The young boy answered honestly, "She is in shame, grandmother. She thinks that you have hated her since that day when she turned her back on you. She has cried every day since we parted," the young boy said as he put his arms around her. "I am worried about her, for she is making herself old with grief."

Ch'idzigyaak sat listening, and her heart went out to her daughter. Yes, she had been very angry. What mother would not be? For all those years she trained her daughter to be strong, only to find the training had been for nothing. Yet, Ch'idzigyaak thought to herself, she is not to be blamed for everything. After all, everyone had participated, and her daughter had acted out of fear. She had been frightened for her son's and mothers lives. It was as simple as that. Ch'idzigyaak also acknowledged that her daughter had been brave to leave the bundle of babiche with the two women. To have left a thing of such value with old ones thought to be near death would have been seen as a foolhardy waste.

Yes, she could forgive her daughter. She could even thank her, for she decided that had it not been for the babiche, they might not have survived. Ch'idzigyaak broke out of her thoughts as she realized that her grandson waited for her to say something. Putting her arms around his shoulders she patted him gently and said, "Tell my daughter that I do not hate her, grandson." Relief flooded the boys face, for he had spent months worrying about his mother and grandmother. Now,

everything was almost the way it once was. Without further encouragement, the boy gave his grandmother an exuberant hug before he bolted out of the shelter and ran all the way home.

He arrived at the camp breathless. Bursting in on his mother, the excited youth said in between gasps, "Mother! Grandmother wishes to see you! She told me there are no hard feelings!" Ozhii Nelii was stunned. She had not expected this, and for a moment her legs became so weak that she had to sit down. Her body trembled, and she looked once more at her son. "Is this true?" she asked, "Yes," Shrub Zhuu replied, and his mother saw that he spoke the truth.

At first, she was afraid to go, for she still felt guilty. But at her son's gentle insistence, Ozhii Nelii gathered enough courage to take the long walk to her mother's camp with her son at her side. When they arrived, the two old women were standing outside the shelter, talking. Sa' saw the visitors first, then Ch'idzigyaak turned to see what caused Sa's silence. When she saw her daughter, her mouth opened but words would not come out. Instead, the women stared at each other until Ch'idzigyaak walked to Ozhii Nelii and embraced her tightly, weeping. All that had stood between them seemed to vanish with the touch.

Sa' stood with her arms around Shrub Zhuu, tearfully watching mother and daughter find the love they thought was lost forever. Then Ch'idzigyaak turned and walked into the tent, returning with a small bundle that she pressed into her daughter's hands. Ozhii Nelii saw that it was babiche. She did not

understand until Ch'idzigyaak leaned forward and whispered something into her daughter's ear. Ozhii Nelii looked surprised a moment, then she, too, smiled. Again the women fell into one another's arms and embraced.

After everyone had been reunited, the chief appointed the two women to honorary positions within the band. At first, people wanted to help the old ones in any way they could, but the women would not allow too much assistance, for they enjoyed their newly found independence. So The People showed their repect for the two women by listening to what they had to say.

More hard times were to follow, for in the cold land of the North it could be no other way, but The People kept their promise. They never again abandoned any elder. They had learned a lesson taught by two whom they came to love and care for until each died a truly happy old woman.